PRAISE FOR **THE LANGUAGE OF LOVE AND OTHER STORIES**

"To an Eskimo, snow is not just a one-noun show. There is *paput*, snow on the ground. Which differs from *piqsirpoq*, drifting snow. Which is not the same as *qimuqsuq*, a snowdrift. And on, and on. And yet, we English speakers give love only one word? Just one syllable? Not according to Ms. Christie, whose remarkable collection of short stories traces the many paths love may take or abandon: grief, joy, confusion, loyalty, frustration, friendship. Thankfully, Nancy Christie is fluent in all of love's many languages, whether between couples, friends, family members, or the person left standing after the love has gone. Allow Ms. Christie, with her documentarian's eye and a poet's pen, to take you by the heart and show you what love is in the real world."

—Alan Sharavsky, author of *Boarding School Bastard*

"*The Language of Love* is a unique collection of short fiction about the various types of love that hits the sweet spot between quirky and heart-rending. Christie's ability to write about the tender and painful moments of love should speak to all types of readers, both young and old: those at the beginning of relationships and those struggling with the end. Her deftness with character and dialogue brings the stories alive and her ability to tuck in life lessons makes this the perfect book to come back to again and again."

—Dawn Reno Langley, author of *Analyzing the Prescotts*

"*The Language of Love* is a beautiful collection by a wonderful storyteller. Nancy Christie explores love in all its forms, from romantic to familial, and in all its stages, from finding it to sustaining it to losing it. Sometimes with humor and often with poignancy, Christie's stories will have the reader examining what they want from their various relationships and what they're willing to give for them."

—Dorothy Rosby, syndicated humor columnist and author

The Language of Love is a deep exploration of the toll and long-lasting effects that caretaking can impose on a relationship, be it parent-child or between lovers. In this collection, Christie deftly moves her characters closer to empathy -- toward each other, but, most importantly, toward themselves."

—Gwen Goodkin, author of *A Place Remote*

"A tribute to the many forms of love, *The Language of Love and Other Stories* presents a thought-provoking collection that looks at life through a lens of irony, compassion, and often humor. Christie's literary prowess once again shines through."

—Ann Henry, author of *Sailing Away from the Moon*

"In her new story collection, *The Language of Love*, Nancy Christie expertly explores love in all its guises. A harried new mother tends simultaneously to her fractious baby and her ailing grandmother. A son realizes that what his aging mother needs is a listening ear. An overburdened woman moves to a small town and becomes involved with a kindly handyman. Poignant, compelling, and clear-eyed, this collection will keep you turning pages until you reach the end."

—Deborah Kalb, author of *Off to Join the Circus*

"*Language of Love and Other Stories* is a real-life account of the different types of love told in a series of short stories. The stories are creative and memorable, and anyone can relate whether it is the love between two supernatural beings, or parent-child-grandparent relationship. Nancy Christie does a fantastic job of pulling readers into her short stories without wasting words. A master of character development, Nancy does a fantastic job of making the characters relatable in a short space of time. Each story takes you on a different emotional experience. For me the underlying theme is patience and grace which is what the world needs right now. These short stories are definitely worth the read and will leave you feeling satisfied."

—Gillian Felix, author of *The Family Portrait Series* and *Adriana*

"This collection of short stories touches on the amazing ways we express love. Ms. Christie puts her characters in situations that drive human emotion...where they burst into laughter, are besieged with happiness, accept their stage in life, deal with grief and gratitude, and so much more. Each story is unique and a joy to read."

—Jan Romes, novelist

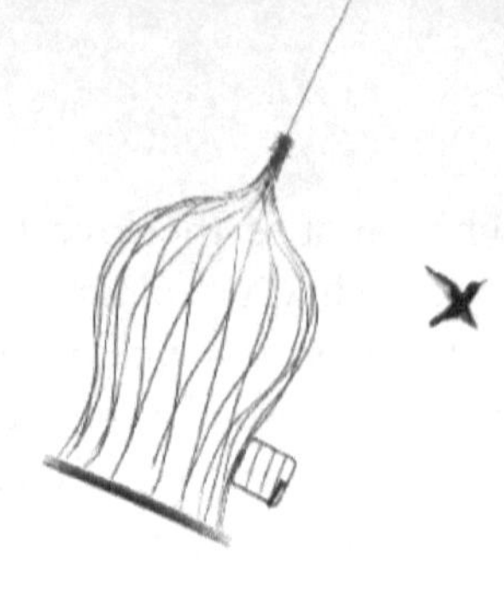

THE LANGUAGE OF

love

NANCY CHRISTIE

"I would not wish any companion in the world but you."
    The Tempest, Act 3 by William Shakespeare

ACKNOWLEDGMENTS

"The Message is Understood" was originally published in *CommuterLit*.

"Henry, Hortense and the Halloween Party was originally published in *CommuterLit*.

"Seeing Jim" was originally published in *The Saturday Evening Post*.

"Doors and Windows" was originally published in *Goat's Milk Magazine*.

"Listen to Me" was originally published in *Edify Fiction*.

"Bingo" was originally published in *Page and Spine*.

"Remember Mama" was originally published in *Talking River* and also appeared in *Peripheral Visions and Other Stories*.

TABLE OF CONTENTS

THE LANGUAGE OF LOVE
AND OTHER STORIES

FRIENDSHIPS

CHARLEY AND THE CUPID CAPER

It was Valentine's Day: my least favorite holiday of the year, the one that stopped me dead in my tracks like a giant heart-shaped stop sign. Years ago (and don't ask me how many years because I don't want to tell you), I believed that Valentine's Day would mean I'd receive a giant bouquet of red roses, an equally giant box of chocolates, and overwhelming amounts of verbal and physical protestations of love.

But after a series of boyfriends who didn't share my beliefs, I had given up on the idea and instead treated the holiday just like any other workday. Which in this case meant coming to work on a frigid Monday morning in my old Chevy without a working heater, hoping that the wonky radiator at Adams Investigation Service would deliver enough warmth to defrost my body, if not my heart that had suffered yet another icepick blow—this time from a new guy who ghosted me after three dates.

All in all, it was a very un-Cupid start to the holiday.

The only positive aspect of the day was that we were scheduled to meet with our latest client, report our findings, and get paid for our efforts. Charley always made it clear that money was due when the results were delivered. This change in policy happened after more than a few clients refused to pay when the outcome wasn't what the client hoped for—the detective agency version of shooting the messenger.

Not that this would be an issue with Patrick Landers. He made it quite apparent at our first meeting that the subject of the background check he requested was someone he thoroughly disliked and distrusted. That he hoped that our investigation would prove his feelings were justified was obvious at the outset. Equally obvious to both our client and us was that, if the information was what he expected, it would most certainly hurt the woman on whose behalf Landers had hired us. But he still put down a healthy deposit to have us look into her "friend" who, he suspected, was no friend at all but a stinker of the first order.

"I'm concerned about the man that Betsy has gotten involved with," Landers said. "His name is Giorgio. Giorgio Leonelli," saying the subject's name as though it left a bad taste in his mouth. He pulled out a folded sheet of paper from his pocket and gave it to Charley, then took a seat. "Here's all I know about him, which isn't much. That's why I'm hiring you. I want to know if my suspicions are correct."

We had done that type of work before, but it was usually for younger, female clients who had doubts about men they met on a dating site or for middle-aged wives who suspected their spouses of cheating on them. But for as long as I'd been working for Charley, this was the first time we'd been hired by a guy well past seventy to do this type of personal investigation.

Charley took the paper and leaned back in his chair, his not inconsiderable bulk making the springs squeak in protest. One of these days, I thought as I moved closer to read over his shoulder, the chair was going to collapse. Then I'd have to call 911 since there was no way I could lift my 300-pound boss off the floor.

Charley looked at the information, then sat forward to make a few notes on his legal pad before asking, "When did all this start?"

"Right after Christmas. Betsy—Betsy Armstrong, in case you need her last name—had joined a Silver Singles group at our church. At first, I thought it was a good idea since Thanksgiving, she'd been keeping to herself more and more. It was all I could do to get her to come out for our regular Friday night dinner and movie."

I looked at our client. "You and this Betsy are a couple?" hoping my tone didn't indicate my thoughts that dating seemed unlikely for people in his age bracket.

But Landers shook his head. "No, no," although I could swear that there was just the faintest blush on his cheeks. "We are just friends," he emphasized. "Anyway, after a few weeks, she started talking about a man named Giorgio. She said he was a widower and how nice he was and how he always walked her out to her car and well, things like that."

After working for Charley for ten years, I had picked up a few tricks, and one of them was to pay as much attention to what a client was doing as much as to what he was saying. In this case, the more Landers talked about this Giorgio, the more his body language indicated his emotions: furrowed brows, narrowed eyes and clenched hands.

"But you didn't trust him." Charley's words were more of a statement than a question.

"No, I didn't!" Landers brought his fist down hard on the arm of his chair. "Sorry. I didn't mean to lose my temper. But Betsy is a sweet, somewhat naïve person who tends to take people at face value. Jack, her late husband—he died five years ago—used to say that if he didn't put his foot down, Betsy would have brought home every stray she found, no matter if it was a cat or a skunk."

Clearly, he put this interloper in the latter category, I noted. "You knew her husband?"

Landers nodded. "Jack and I worked together before our retirement, and my late wife Mary and Betsy were in the same garden club. And we all belonged to the same church. When my wife passed away, they would have me over for dinner every Friday evening, and then when Jack died two years later, well, Betsy and I kept up the tradition, only we went out instead. And I was happy for her when she joined that group. I thought she'd make some new friends."

Another silence, then Charley cleared his throat—a sign that he wanted to make a point.

"So far, you haven't given us any reason, aside from your personal feelings, for wanting us to check into Giorgio. We could run the basic background check, but why?"

"Because he's been asking her for money!" His words came out in an angry rush. "The first time was when he took her out to dinner at the Venetian Café."

I knew the place, not that I had ever eaten there, given that the price they charged for a bowl of spaghetti and two meatballs was beyond my meager budget. Besides, I suspected the valet service would balk at parking my twenty-year-old car next to the Lincolns and Caddys that filled the lot.

"I asked her how the evening went—it was her first real date since she lost Jack—and she said fine except that Giorgio was so embarrassed when the waiter came with the bill, and he realized he had left his wallet at home. She paid, of course, and said that Giorgio promised to pay her back. But when I asked her later if he had, she changed the subject. Then there was the day trip the group went on to museums and art galleries. Betsy asked me if I wanted to go, but I was having a root canal, so I had to pass. She said not to worry, Giorgio was going anyway."

The expression on his face indicated that far from reassuring him, Betsy's response was a major source of unease, possibly even exceeding the impending dental appointment.

"Later she told me that there had been some mix-up with the reservations—she blamed the trip coordinator—and when they boarded the bus, the person in charge said Giorgio's name wasn't on the reservation list and he couldn't go unless he paid right then and there. Of course his credit card wouldn't work—

Betsy said something about a problem with the scanner—and she had the cash so she paid for him."

I could see the pulse pounding in his temple and hoped the old guy wouldn't stroke out while he was sitting there. I glanced at Charley, but his eyes were on our client, who took a deep breath before continuing.

"But the latest incident was the last straw. According to Betsy, Giorgio's condo—which she'd never been to, by the way—was being remodeled, and he asked if he could stay in her spare bedroom until renovations were through. He said"— his tone making it clear how little weight he gave to Giorgio's words—"it would only be for a week or two. And that he'd be happy to pay her. But she told me she had no intention of charging him. 'He's been so nice to me,' was her explanation when I questioned her about it, and then she changed the subject. Again."

He shifted in his chair. "I don't want to get into a fight with Betsy over this guy, so I thought if I found out a little more about him and if he turned out to be what I think he is, then I'd give the information to her and let her make up her own mind. I just don't want to see her hurt. Or taken to the cleaners."

It was admirable that Landers was willing to part with cold hard cash on behalf of his friend, although I couldn't help wondering if there was something more to it, especially since every time he mentioned her name, his cheeks got even redder. But before I could follow up this line of thought, Charley handed him our standard contract to sign, took his deposit— three one-hundred-dollar bills, I noticed—and said, "We should have the results in a few weeks—say, by February 14. My assistant" nodding in my direction "will set up a time for you to come in and get the report. And pay the balance due," he added, and I breathed a sigh of relief, knowing the pitiful state of our bank account.

Once Landers left, Charley divvied up the tasks pertaining to this new—and thus far only—client. He'd do the traditional background check, which involved searching through online databases to find out about any criminal records and marriages and divorces, along with other information that people think is hidden but, thanks to the internet, is readily available if you knew where and how to find it.

My job was to troll through the social media platforms and dating sites (of which I was sadly all too familiar) looking for anything that might be linked to this Giorgio person. And thanks to the digital pictures of this guy that our client emailed us—I suspected he had followed the couple on their outings to get it, but I didn't ask—I would have another way to do my search.

I started with dating sites targeting seniors, figuring that if this was Giorgio's MO, he was bound to be on at least one of them hunting for more victims. My first stop was at Never Too Late For Love. Luckily, I didn't have to create an account, not that I would have objected to using the company credit card in the interest of research. All they wanted was my gender, the gender I was hoping to connect with, my first name and my birth date. I plugged in female, male, "Charlene" and Charley's birth date, deciding to make my boss a part of the process. Then I pressed "Submit" and waited to see if Giorgio's face showed up. It didn't take long before the Latin Lothario appeared, with the screen name "Looking for Love." His bio listed him as an award-winning artist who moved to the States after losing his wife to an unnamed disease and was now looking for "companionship."

Uh, huh. I thought, scanning his list of interests: opera, plays, gourmet dining, and the obligatory "walks along the beach at sunset." Just the thing that would catch an older woman's interest.

Next up was the Silver Passion site, featuring images of older women wearing the least they could get away with without the site being rated "R" and men with unbuttoned shirts or in some cases, no shirts at all.

I started my search again, first plugging in my fictitious information and then seeing who popped up that fit my criteria: male, fifty and older, status: single, divorced, or widowed. It didn't take long for a parade of men to scroll across the screen. Who knew so many unattached guys couldn't find women to date?

I clicked on a guy who looked like an older Sean Connery. He's not bad, I decided, and then chose another who was a dead-ringer for George Clooney. Both said they were available, and both were looking for women who longed to bring "long dormant embers to full fire," as the Clooney look-alike put it.

Just for a minute, I thought of signing up for the site, even though I was not quite in the required age range (although who would know, I wondered) but then stopped myself. You're here to research, not catch a Sugar Daddy, I told myself sternly, and regretfully I closed the Connery and Clooney screens and went back to my assignment.

This time, I had to scroll through four screens before Giorgio appeared, his image identifying him with the moniker "Ready to Cook In Your Kitchen." It was the same picture but a different bio. In this one, Giorgio claimed to be a gourmet chef who had owned a line of Michelin-starred restaurants on the Amalfi Coast (natch!), but after retiring came to the United States for a complete change of lifestyle and to find passionate love. His desire was to "cook for a woman who appreciated good food and good wine and"—(no surprise)—"walks along the beach at sunset as well as other pleasurable after-dinner activities." It didn't take a college degree to figure out what he meant, I thought.

In the interest of being thorough, I decided to visit one more, and chose Golden Hearts, marketed as "the place where those in the prime of their lives can find companionship and fun." I sent "Charlene" on the hunt, and there he was again: the same picture but yet another screen name and bio.

"Hmmm," I murmured to myself as I read his information, "let's see who you are this time."

If nothing else, I had to give Giorgio props for being creative. If I ever had to look for another job, I might hire him to do my résumé. In lieu of a clever screen name, he had settled for "George" and identified himself as a retired accountant for a nonprofit organization who just wanted someone to "have fun with. I like going to farmer's markets and church festivals as well as engaging in volunteer activities that benefit the community. I also enjoy walks along the beach at sunset. If this sounds like something you'd like to do, please connect."

I sighed. If I had any lingering dreams that romance still existed in this digital, only-make-a-virtual-connection age, this research killed them.

I filed the screenshots and the URLs from all three sites under "Client: Landers, P" and then uploaded his image to my favorite search engine to see where else our boy Giorgio might show up. In seconds there he was, on a social media site that catered to the Medicare club. But while his "About Me" page was notably short on personal info, his "My Favorite Pix" more than made up for it with a seemingly endless array of images.

There was a cherry-red Corvette with the caption "My newest ride" underneath, followed by a beach house backlit by a gorgeous sunset labeled "My getaway." Other pictures: a three-story mansion ("My house"), a corral with three horses ("My pets"), and a 1939 Triumph motorcycle—a fact I knew only because he identified it under the label "My toy."

Other images followed: several of cruise ships captioned with various destinations: "My Bahama vacation," "My Alaskan cruise," "On my way to European hotspots" as well as trains with names such as Deutsche Bahn AG and Trenitalia that were intended to give the false impression that he was a world-class traveler.

More screenshots, more web addresses—it was rapidly adding up to a damning collection of lies and false identities. And by the time of our next meeting, the two of us had amassed enough info to justify our client's suspicions. Unfortunately, I didn't make it to the office on time, and instead arrived barely fifteen minutes before Landers was due to arrive—a fact that Charley didn't overlook, since that meant I was also a half hour past the time the agency opened for business.

"You're late."

"Yeah, I know," I said, stomping the snow off my boots before hanging my coat in the closet. "But Charley, you know they never plow the apartment's parking lot before nine. And the roads weren't salted either. And my car needs new tires. And—"

Charley held up his hand to stop me from continuing my litany of what I considered legitimate justifications. "Never mind about all that. Landers called and said he was bringing Betsy with him. I guess he figured having a neutral third party deliver the news would be better all the way around."

Great. Nothing like passing the buck and making us the bearer of bad news. But before I could answer, the office door opened, revealing our client and a female I assumed was Betsy. I don't know what I expected—a frail old woman using a wheelchair?—but when I saw her, I understood why Landers colored up every time he mentioned her name.

For an old lady, she was darned cute, slim of build with dimpled cheeks, a bright smile, and a lively way of walking that belied her age. She reminded me of an Angora cat I once used to pet-sit: delicate-boned with sparkling blue eyes and silky white hair, yet full of playful energy. And affectionate, too, judging by the way she linked her arm with his, leading me to wonder if she might have more than a little fondness for him.

"Mr. Adams, this is Betsy Armstrong. Betsy, this is Charley Adams, and his assistant."

"Terry McCallister," I said. "Please take a seat," positioning a second chair in front of Charley's desk. I decided to place myself behind the couple, partly because the radiator was giving off a comforting blast of hot air that warmed my backside and partly because I didn't want to watch that smile fade from her face when Charley confronted her with the reality of who and what Giorgio was: a sneaky, despicable modern-day gigolo who was out to get what he could from unwary females of any age.

"I thought Patrick was taking me out to breakfast but instead here we are!" she said, giving her partner a teasing look before patting his hand with her well-manicured fingers. "Not that I mind, really," settling herself in the chair as though it was a well-padded throne instead of a more-than-dilapidated piece of office furniture. "Besides, I never met a private investigator before!"

Charley cleared his throat twice—never a good sign. Once meant he wanted to talk, but twice was an indication that what he was going to say wasn't anything good. "Yes, well, from what I understand from our client, the information he had me acquire for him might be of some interest to someone else. You, that is."

He looked down at his notes as though searching for a way to share the ugly details that wouldn't hurt her.

I was surprised. Charley rarely showed emotion when it came to client meetings but in this case, he seemed to be struggling with his feelings. Luckily, our client rescued him.

"What he means," said Landers, pausing to take a deep breath, "is that I had him investigate Giorgio. Because I didn't trust him. And I didn't want you to get hurt. Or be taken advantage of. Or, well, anything like that," finishing quickly.

"You had him investigate Giorgio."

Her words came out with slow deliberation, each one given equal weight. If Betsy was a cat, her fur would be standing straight up at this point. She gave him a sharp look before repositioning her chair just a fraction away from his. Small as it was, the movement spoke volumes. "May I ask by what right you shared my private life with a stranger?"

I knew that tone. It meant things were going very badly for Landers, and if he didn't say something quickly, their friendship was headed for the rocks. Unfortunately, he didn't seem to have anything worth saying. So, before their relationship boat capsized, I stepped in.

I came around to stand behind Charley so I could see her face as I threw in my two cents. "I think what he meant was that, based on the long-time friendship and affection he has for you, and knowing what a kind and trusting person you are, he simply wanted to make sure that anyone you spent time with was worthy of you."

I was proud of myself for coming up with that on the spur of the moment. And after all, what woman wouldn't want to know that someone worried about her?

What woman? Well, apparently *this* woman, since when I finished, she gathered up her handbag and rose to her feet, pointedly turning her back to her companion.

"Thank you for your time. I'd like to leave now." She looked at me. "Will you call me a cab?"

I glanced at Landers, but he had his head down, his body one big lump of misery. Men, I thought. They start something never thinking how it might turn out, and when it all goes south, they don't know what to do so they do nothing. I sighed and moved my hand toward the phone on Charley's desk, but he stopped me before I could lift the receiver.

"I understand that you're upset," Charley said gently. "But I think it would be wise of you to hear the results of our report. Then, if you still want to leave, my assistant will be happy to drive you home."

Betsy paused for a moment, then sat down, still ignoring Landers. "I'll listen to what you have to say but it isn't going to change my mind about anything."

Charley handed her the report. "Perhaps it would be better if you read it for yourself. Then, if you have any questions, we'll do our best to answer them."

She began reading, the silence only broken by the sound of her flipping through all ten pages. There was enough incriminating evidence, complete with screen captures and images, to convict the man of, at the very least, concealment and, at the worst, of outright deception. But, as I knew from my own experience, sometimes we just don't want to see the truth, even when it's presented in stark black and white.

I watched her face and body, hoping I could get some indication of her thoughts. But she kept a firm hold on her reactions, the only giveaway a slight tightening of her lips. What she couldn't control, however, was the hand gripping the papers. It shook, ever so slightly.

Finished with her review, Betsy put the papers on Charley's desk, giving them the very slightest push away from her.

"Do you have any questions?" Charley asked.

"Just one. Why did you do this?" she asked, turning to our client who still kept his head down.

Silence.

"Patrick," and she touched him gently. "I need to know why you spent your money on this report."

"Because I care about you," he mumbled.

At his response, I thought I saw the faintest smile on her lips.

"As a friend?" she prompted, and he finally lifted his head to look at her.

"No, well, yes," he stammered. "I mean, of course as a friend but damn it, Betsy, it's been five years since Jack died and well, I mean…" and there he stopped, obviously unsure if he should go on.

"Yes, it has been five years since he died, and you have been a wonderful companion to me, very supportive especially in the beginning," she said. "But after a while, I started to wonder if that was all we would be: two people who had lost our spouses and spent time together as a way of getting through the loneliness. Or, if there was a possibility that we could be more to each other."

She stopped there, and I found myself holding my breath. It was our client's turn to say or do something to fix the situation, but I wasn't sure if he was up to the task. Men, I thought. They could be so stupid sometimes.

But in this case, I did Landers an injustice. "I'd like to be more than just a friend, Betsy," moving closer to her and taking her hand in his. "I didn't realize how much until you started seeing—" he paused for a moment, obviously choosing his words with care before saying, "that guy. And if you still want to spend time with him, I won't stand in your way. I just think you deserve better."

"Better? You mean, better like you?" Betsy questioned, but the smile she gave him was full of encouragement.

"Yes, like me!" and he gently pulled her to her feet. "What do you say we go have breakfast and talk?" and she nodded.

Without another word, the two moved toward the door, and I held my breath, hoping Charley wouldn't interrupt the romantic moment with something as prosaic as a request for payment. Fortunately, he didn't. He just sat there and watched the two of them—Landers opening the door with a flourish and Betsy smiling up at him—and then, once the door closed, handed me the invoice.

"Here, kid, mail this to his house. I don't think he'll be a problem when it comes to paying. After all, he got more than he expected," giving me a grin.

"That's it?" I asked. "I mean, it worked out well for the two of them, but what about this Giorgio guy? He's bound to try it again with someone else!"

"Oh, I don't think so," said Charley, picking up the phone and tapping a number I recognized as belonging to our local PD. "Hey, Freddie, it's Charley. I have some information about a guy that might be of interest to the team working fraud cases. I'll email it over and you can pass it on. I'd like to see this guy get what's coming to him."

I couldn't hear what Freddie answered, but whatever it was, it was good enough for Charley. "Okay, great. See you at Friday's poker game!" and he ended the call.

"Satisfied now?" Charley said, and when I nodded, he lumbered to his feet. "Then get your coat and let's go. I'm treating you to breakfast at Big Ben's Buffet. Happy Valentine's Day, kid!"

PARENT AND CHILD

MAMA

"Can you say 'Mama'?"

Juliette heard the note of frustration in her voice and hated it. This wasn't supposed to be a contest. She was just doing what all mothers did when they were trying to teach their babies to talk.

But she kept on. "Come on, Sherry, can you say 'Mama'—just once? Please?"

She felt the old woman edge closer, caught her sour old-person smell, and tried to move farther away, ashamed of herself for doing it. This was her grandmother, after all.

"Baby? Baby?" The gnarled hands reached out and Juliette tightened her grip. The old woman—her grandmother, she reminded herself—couldn't be trusted. Just yesterday she had dropped one of Juliette's treasured statues, a memento from their honeymoon in Greece, and it shattered into a thousand pieces.

"Baby?" and then a string of incomprehensible sounds that these days passed for words. Soon, they told her, her grandmother would most likely lose her ability to speak at all. The progression of the disease, while unpredictable, was inevitable.

Juliette stood up, shifting just enough to place her body between the infant and her grandmother. "It's bedtime,

Sherry," she said, not so much to the baby as to the old woman. "Mama is going to put you to bed now for your nap." And then, one more time, "Can you say 'Mama'?" knowing as she did so that the response she wanted would not be forthcoming.

She left the room, hoping her grandmother would stay behind. She wanted—no, she needed—a break from the never-ending monitoring that seemed to have been going on forever, but in reality only started early this morning and would, in fact, come to a close sometime tomorrow afternoon.

"It's just for one night," her mother had explained on the phone. "It's just a simple procedure, nothing really. But they told me that I wouldn't be up to taking care of Grandma until the next day."

Juliette was sure her mother was waiting for her to say, "No problem, Mom. Grandma can come here. I'd love to have her," but she held back. It *was* a problem, and she *didn't* want her here. She had enough to do. No one had told her how much time and energy a new baby could suck up. She drained Juliette's spirits like she drained Juliette's breasts, and in both cases, never seemed to reach a satiation point but just demanded more and more and more.

And with Patrick now doing long hauls across the country, she had spent most of the past few months alone with the baby. But even when her husband was home, Juliette was still the one who handled most of the baby's needs: feeding, bathing, rocking her to sleep, and sometimes endlessly walking the floor with her when the colic took hold—the colic, the doctor had said, that should have stopped two months ago but hadn't yet. Was it so much to ask that her daughter at least try to speak her name?

"Please, Juliette" and she caught that note of desperation in her mother's voice.

It was the same undercurrent that she heard so often in her own when Patrick would call and say he had run into delays on the return trip. And so she sighed and agreed, well aware that her mother knew that she was doing it out of duty, not desire.

With the baby now settled in her crib for what Juliette hoped would be a long nap, she went to the kitchen to make an afternoon snack for her grandmother.

Feeding the old woman was another challenge. At lunch, her grandmother refused to swallow even one bite of her meatloaf or vegetables and instead pushed the peas around on the dish until they rolled, one by one, onto the table and then to the floor. Frustrated, Juliette had taken the dish away and then brought her crackers smeared with peanut butter.

But that didn't work either. Her grandmother picked up each small square, her fingers turning it over and over as though searching for something, and then closed her hand tightly, the spread oozing out and the crumbs sticking to her skin. By the time Juliette had cleaned up the mess, her own meal had grown cold, and the baby needed to be changed again.

Out of ideas, Juliette reached for one of the liquid supplements her mother had given her: a carefully blended mix of vitamins, minerals, and protein in drink form.

"Just hold it up to her lips," her mother had told her. "She usually takes sips, but sometimes you have to coax her."

Coax her, like Juliette had been coaxing Sherry every time it was time for her to nurse. You would think by now the baby would have taken to the breast, but even after six months, feeding time was a never-ending battle: Juliette trying to get Sherry to suck and Sherry obstinately pushing the nipple away as if it was something unpleasant, until she finally gave in and latched on.

But even then it wasn't the soothing, mothering experience Juliette had read would occur, but a painful encounter: Sherry's hard gums grinding against Juliette's tender skin while Juliette, holding back tears, resisted the urge to free herself. When the pediatrician said she could start solid food and even suggested switching to a bottle, Juliette jumped at the recommendations, even though she was secretly ashamed of the relief she felt.

She poured some of the beverage into a sippy cup, not trusting her grandmother to hold a glass, and then guided the old woman to the couch.

"Here, Grandma," and she held it up to her mouth.

But her grandmother kept her lips tightly closed, pushed at Juliette's hand, and then turned her head away.

"Grandma, you have to have something," with a note of desperation in her voice. How did her mother do it, day after day, she wondered, as the battle between them continued: Juliette trying to get the cup to her grandmother's lips and her grandmother dodging her at every turn.

Her mother—and what was the procedure she was having? She had been circumspect when Juliette first asked, brushing it off as "a routine exam. The doctor just wants to check out a few things and this is the only way to do it."

But now, as she struggled to get her grandmother to drink, Juliette worried that there was more to it than that. What if there was something wrong, something major—like cancer? What if she was really ill? What if—and Juliette's hand started to tremble—what if she's going to die? What will I do without her?

As the thought came into her mind, Juliette closed her eyes and, in that moment, her grandmother slapped the cup from her grip. The cup hit the floor, the lid snapped off, and liquid spread across the carpet.

"Grandma!" Her words, louder than she intended, were driven by a mix of fear and anger. "Now look what you did!"

She ran to the kitchen for paper towels, but just then, Sherry started to cry. Too soon—it was too soon for her to be awake. She should have slept for hours yet. Juliette dropped the towels on the counter and turned to head toward the nursery, nearly bumping into her grandmother who had come up noiselessly behind her.

"Baby," her grandmother muttered. "Baby," again.

Juliette took a deep breath, trying to get her emotions under control. "Yes, Grandma, I hear the baby," guiding her back to the living room. "Just stay here, and I'll make you something to eat after I change her."

Her grandmother obediently sat down on the couch, ankles crossed, hands in her lap, as though she was a well-behaved ten-year-old girl instead of a ninety-year-old woman rapidly losing control of everything: her body, her emotions, her mind. Then, she smiled at Juliette, and just for a moment, Juliette saw not this person but a much younger version, the grandmother that Juliette used to visit when she was a child.

She would spend days at her grandmother's house—sometimes helping in the garden, sometimes baking with her in the kitchen. Each morning, her grandmother would make hot cocoa with marshmallows and cinnamon toast for breakfast, and each evening, her grandmother would read to her before tucking her into bed. And if at times Juliette tracked mud into the house or spilled her milk on the floor, her grandmother would just smile and then patiently clean it up.

Patience—where had the old woman found it, Juliette wondered now, as she went to change the baby's diaper and put her in a fresh onesie, a onesie that only too soon would be stained with cereal and spit-up. And her own mother, too, whose life was now constrained by the needs and wants of an old woman whose moods were as mercurial as the weather.

And why, she thought as she returned to the living room, had that patience not been handed down to me?

"There, all done," settling herself in the rocker next to the couch. Maybe she could soothe her baby back to sleep. Maybe

Sherry would close her eyes and Juliette would be able to slip her back into the crib so she could clean up the drink (now undoubtedly soaking into the padding) and find something else to feed her grandmother.

Or maybe the three of them would stay right where they were as the minutes of the day and of Juliette's life inexorably ticked away.

For a brief period, it seemed like Sherry would be quiet. But then it started: her tiny face screwed up in a grimace and her eyes opened to stare at her mother in bewilderment, as though asking why everything hurt and why her mother didn't make it stop. Then the screaming started: an ear-splitting rise and fall accompanied by a deluge of tears, and it was all Juliette could do to not match her scream for scream, tear for tear.

"Baby." Her grandmother had shifted closer to the rocker, leaning over the sofa's arm to stroke the infant's cheek. And whether she was surprised by the sudden touch or just experiencing a lull in the cramping, Sherry stopped crying and looked wide-eyed at the old, wrinkled face staring down at her.

"Baby," but then the stroking stopped, and her grandmother pushed herself up off the cushions and went toward the front door.

"Grandma, come back."

But the old woman didn't heed the call and Juliette was forced to shift the baby to her shoulder and go after her grandmother. The last time, the old woman had opened the door, and it took all Juliette's strength to pull her back inside.

Dragging her with one hand while she held the baby with the other, Juliette managed to get the three of them into the kitchen.

"Here. Sit here," pushing her grandmother with slightly more force than necessary into the chair farthest from the doorway, before putting Sherry in her swing. It was the newest addition to the steadily increasing inventory of nursery items that took over the house and depleted their budget. Patrick had brought it home from his last run and set it up in the kitchen.

"There," he told Juliette after he strapped the baby in the cushioned seat. "Now she can watch you while you work."

He was pleased with himself for thinking of it, Juliette knew, but what he didn't understand was that she wanted—needed!—at least a few hours away from their child, the housework, the endless calls on her time and attention. But she couldn't tell him that. What kind of mother would he think she was? What kind of mother would need a break from the baby they had both wanted—a baby who refused to acknowledge her by calling her "Mama"?

And why did it matter after all, she thought wearily as she guided the pacifier into the baby's mouth. She was Sherry's mother. She didn't need her daughter to say that word to make it real, even though there were some days when Juliette didn't feel it was real at all.

Exhausted, she slumped into the chair. She should clean up the mess in the living room, but she couldn't leave her grandmother alone with the baby. She should come up with something else to feed her grandmother but was at a loss what to try even if the old woman would take it. She should wash the breakfast and lunch dishes, throw in a load of laundry, brush her teeth, and comb her hair. Instead, Juliette sat there, head in her hands.

"Baby."

Juliette looked at her grandmother and then her child. The two of them were staring at each other, and then Sherry smiled at the old woman as though recognizing a kindred spirit.

Had her daughter smiled at her today? Juliette asked herself, but she couldn't remember. It seemed like every time she looked at her child, all she saw were tears or frowns or tightly closed eyes as though she couldn't bear to look at the woman who had brought her into the world which, thus far, had treated her so badly.

But she would smile at Patrick. Every time her husband came home, he would lift her into his arms and make silly faces at her, and Sherry would gurgle and coo. But when Juliette tried that, more often than not, the baby turned her head away as though searching for someone else.

Not always, though, she told herself. There were those few treasured moments when she and Sherry would sit together in the rocker, the baby's head against her breast, her tiny lips softly parted as she slept. Those were the times when Juliette felt like a mother, when successful mothering itself seemed to be within her reach.

The peace never lasted long, just like this quiet interlude didn't last for more than a few minutes. Sherry started to cry at almost the same moment her grandmother struggled to get out of the chair.

"No!" The word exploded from Juliette, whether at the baby or her grandmother, it didn't matter. She pressed her grandmother's body back into the chair, pressed the pacifier back into Juliette's mouth from where it had escaped, and then left the table. It was too early for dinner, but she had to make her grandmother something to eat.

A quick version of French toast, she decided, first dipping the bread into the milk-and-egg mixture before frying the slices in a pan. And for once, the idea was a good one. Her grandmother ate two of the pieces, and Juliette finished the third, realizing that she hadn't eaten since last night. Often, her own mealtimes went by the wayside when Patrick wasn't home.

"Okay, then," and Juliette wiped her grandmother's mouth and fingers clean. "That's done. Now what shall we do?"

"Baby?" and Juliette nodded.

"Yes, Grandma, you and I will take the baby into the living room and put on television, and then, and then…" but she couldn't decide what to do next. There were so many tasks that needed to be completed, but she was too exhausted to even formulate the order in which they should be done, let alone summon the energy to do them.

They can wait, she decided, as she sat the baby in the playpen next to the couch before returning to guide her grandmother into the room. They can all wait. I just need some peace.

And for the next several hours, Juliette found it. Her grandmother dozed on the couch and Sherry in the playpen, the muted sound of the television occasionally punctuated by a gentle snore from one of the two—Juliette wasn't sure which and didn't really care. She took advantage of the break to do a quick clean-up of the spill on the carpet, before lying down on the floor, pillow under her head. And by the time dusk had fallen, she had rested sufficiently to be ready for the evening's activities: meals, baths, and bedtime.

I can do this, she told herself, as she mixed up the baby cereal for her daughter. I'm a good mother. I can handle all this, she thought, as she cut the hamburger into small bites for her grandmother to eat.

But the cereal came out of Sherry's mouth as quickly as Juliette fed it to her, and the dinner plate somehow ended up on the floor, sending ground meat bits all over: a portent of the frustrations to come as the hours-long evening routine began. Another round of colic, followed by diaper changes and bottle-feeding. And with each task, Juliette tried anew to encourage her daughter to say the one word that, for some reason, she thought would make all the difference: "Mama."

But Sherry would only look at her uncomprehendingly and then babble phrases of her own making.

Maybe tomorrow, Juliette told herself, as she settled her daughter in her crib, unsure why it mattered so much but only knowing that it did.

Then it was her grandmother's turn: Juliette spoon-feeding her yogurt and bananas for her evening snack, then helping her out of her clothes and into her nightgown. She washed the wrinkled face and guided her grandmother's hand as the old woman brushed what was left of her teeth.

Finally, Juliette led her to the spare room. There, she tucked the old woman in and closed the door, before making her way to her own room to crawl into her bed only to stare sleeplessly at the ceiling. She wondered if she would ever get better at parenting or if this was just a portent of what was to come: two-year-old tantrums she couldn't manage, teenage rebellion that she couldn't control.

Did all new mothers feel like this or was it just her? Was mothering something she simply wasn't capable of, a talent she didn't possess, an emotional gift that she lacked?

The fears banged themselves around inside her head until it ached from the repercussions, and resignedly, Juliette rose to get an aspirin. That's when she heard it: a series of soft cries and moans.

It wasn't Sherry, Juliette thought. By now, she knew the way her baby sounded when she was crying, and these weren't the whimpers of a six-month-old. Just to be certain, she peeked into her daughter's room, but Sherry was fast asleep, her tiny body relaxed and peaceful.

Her grandmother? Juliette opened the door to the room where her grandmother was sleeping—*should* be sleeping—and saw the old woman twisting and turning on the bed. And then it came again, the sound of muffled weeping.

"Grandma, what's wrong?" gently touching her shoulder. But the crying went on, a heartbreaking lament all the worse because her grandmother was asleep.

Was she having a nightmare? Juliette shook her just enough to bring her to wakefulness. But even then, even when her grandmother finally opened her eyes to stare up at her, the tears continued.

"Don't cry, Grandma. Everything is okay," and Juliette climbed into bed to lie down behind her, pulling her fragile body closer. "Don't cry," she repeated, stroking her grandmother's hair. "I'm here."

Gradually the old woman's cries subsided and then she turned to face Juliette who smiled at her.

"Go to sleep now," Juliette whispered, wiping away the tears with her fingers.

Her grandmother smiled back and then reached up to touch Juliette's cheek. "Mama."

CLAIRE JULIANA

It's only 10 a.m., and I'm already on my second pot of coffee. Not ordinarily being a coffee drinker, I think—no, I'm certain—that it must have something to do with Claire Juliana and the flu.

Claire Juliana is my sixteen-year-old daughter: long-limbed, curly-haired, fair-skinned. When she was born, I gave her a beautiful name to help compensate for all the things I wouldn't be able to give her: dancing lessons, a stay-at-home mother, a father.

But she informed me just last week that her name was, in her words, "just too gross! I want to be called 'C.J.' from now on."

All this was delivered in the challenging tone she has only recently perfected. Every request (a loose term for the demands she frequently voices) is delivered in this same tone, with the unspoken assumption that I'll argue the point with her.

And if I do, I lose—one way or the other.

The books say this is a normal developmental stage but offer minimal advice on how to keep my temper and sanity. Overnight, it seems my beautiful Claire Juliana has turned into an angry stranger, and I'm trapped in a house with someone who behaves as if she doesn't love me, and worse, won't let me love her.

Just three days ago, she demanded a lock on her bedroom door. Not that she was doing anything wrong in there, you understand. It was just that she wanted some privacy. The same child who once insisted on sleeping in my bed now wants to enter her room and lock me outside.

I agreed to the lock. What choice did I have? I installed it the very next evening. And the third night, when the virus began, I had to fumble with a bobby pin to get the door unlocked while Claire Juliana shivered and retched on the other side.

It could have been much worse. There could have been a fire, and she would have been trapped in her room. Or she could have passed out from the fever. Or I could have failed to get the door unlocked. All those worries mothers are so expert at imagining filled my mind, but one look at her flushed cheeks and I held the lecture until she was better.

All that day, Claire Juliana threw up every bit of food she'd eaten in the last forty-eight hours, and then some. The fever turned her shining brown hair into a tangled mass, and as I gently combed out the knots, I couldn't help wondering how long it had been since I last brushed her hair. When did I stop? When did she become old enough to comb it herself?

I didn't know. Like all seemingly insignificant events in a child's maturing process, it only became important after the fact—after you realize that what was once a chore had taken on new importance as a milestone the child raced past when you weren't watching.

Most of that day I spent in her room, handing her juice, cold cloths, and pain reliever. She was too sick to care that I called her "Claire Juliana," too sick to protest an invalid diet, sick enough to call out "Mommy" on those rare times when I left her side.

And even though I hated seeing her so wretched, there was a certain comfort in knowing that she wanted me, needed me—that for now, she was once again my little girl who would accept all the comforting without protest. Last night, when the fever ran the highest and I was too exhausted to sit up any longer, I brought her into my room—all ninety-seven pounds, five-feet-two of her—and laid down with her, rubbing her back until she dropped off into an exhausted sleep.

She's sleeping still, while I sit here in the kitchen and drink yet another cup of coffee, in the hopes that the caffeine will compensate for the lack of sleep. My mother had called a few minutes earlier, supposedly to check on Claire Juliana. But I sense she is really checking on me—asking if I've slept, if I've eaten.

And instead of responding in the half-irritated tone I've often used with her, I was overwhelmed with the need to lay my head in her lap and let her handle everything: my exhaustion, Claire Juliana's fever, the pile of sheets stinking of sweat and vomit thrown haphazardly into the laundry room sometime during the endless night.

But I said I was fine, and then, surprising us both, I told my mother how much I appreciated her concern, how much it meant to me. And, after I hung up the phone, I thought back to all the times I pushed her away, wanting to do things my way and live life on my own terms, how many times I thoughtlessly caused her pain. I marveled at her ability to forgive and forget and hoped that ability had been passed down to me.

I finish my coffee, wondering if Claire Juliana and I will ever reach that point where I can be her mother without her pushing me away—when she will let me hold her and love her without struggling in my arms like some wild bird, trying to be free.

I suppose that's the way it should be. Inch by painful inch, the child tears loose from the mother, and all the love in the world won't stop her from growing up, growing away. I know that. Intellectually, I understand the maturing process. And I truly want to see my daughter as a healthy, independent woman, able to face the future standing on her own two feet.

But some small part of me—the selfish part, I suspect—will still be waiting for those rare few times when my little girl needs me, when I will be called "Mommy" once again by my beautiful Claire Juliana.

THE FERRIS WHEEL

"Come on, Daddy!"

Melodie pulled at his arm with more strength than one would expect from a nine-year-old. Or was she ten?

He tried to remember how many candles were on the cake his sister had brought last week. Thank God for Susan. He had completely lost track of the day, and when she had called to check about the arrangements, he was embarrassed to admit that he hadn't made any.

"I'll bring the cake, Adam," Susan had said soothingly. "Chocolate with chocolate frosting, right?" and he agreed, not sure if it was his daughter's favorite but relieved to have someone else make the decision.

But he couldn't continue to push everything off on Susan. Or the teachers. Or the after-school monitor. Or the babysitter. Some things he had to do—those things that Carla always did. And riding the Ferris wheel was one of them.

Carla and Melodie loved riding the Ferris wheel at the small county fair and happily stood in line for what seemed like an eternity just for that brief experience. And each time, when it was over and Melodie disembarked from the passenger car, she would run to him with her face alight with joy.

"You should have come, Daddy! It's fun! You'd love it!"

Carla stood there smiling while Adam shook his head. She knew that he wouldn't get in the car for love or money. He hated heights and he hated not being in control even more. She understood that, like she had understood so many other things about him.

"It's okay, Melodie," she would tell their daughter as she relieved him of the child's backpack and her handbag. "Somebody has to hold our stuff and Daddy said he would," sparing his pride while she justified his decision.

He loved her for that. He loved her for so many reasons. *Had* loved her—or did love stop when there was no one there to give it to?

"Please?" and he looked at his daughter, her blue eyes so like Carla's, the dimple on her right cheek a match for the one that Carla had, that he could still see traces of even when her face was drawn and almost skeletal. Was that what finally drove him to buy the tickets and, his daughter's hand in his, take their place in line?

"Your turn," and Adam stepped forward and, with sweaty hands, guided his daughter into the car before taking his seat beside her. The operator lowered the front bar, then stepping back to the controls, pushed the lever forward.

The ride began its revolution, and instinctively Adam shut his eyes but then forced himself to open them again. He was in charge. He had to be aware, pay attention, keep watch on his daughter in case something went wrong. Although, even if it did, even if one of the bars let go or the electrical system failed, there was nothing he could do.

He would be helpless—again.

"We could try another round of chemo, but I have to be clear. The prognosis isn't good," the oncologist had said to both of them last September.

But while Carla seemed to understand the news, all Adam could hear was a buzzing that grew louder and louder until it drowned out everything else in the hospital room.

He never even heard Carla tell the doctor her decision. He knew what it was, of course. She had told him the night before that last, and what ended up to be her final, surgery. But still, he should have heard it.

"Daddy, look! I can see our house from here!"

Melodie jostled his arm and he grabbed at the bar in front of them, irrationally afraid that he would fall.

"Stop it!" Adam said angrily, but then, seeing his daughter's startled reaction to his tone as though he had slapped her, he forced a smile to his face. "Daddy's afraid of heights, you know," trying to make it a joke.

But it didn't work. He could tell by the way she turned away. He had failed her. This was supposed to be a fun father-daughter time as well as an indication that he could fill the place of her mother. But not only had he robbed her of that comfort, he hadn't even acted as a father—just a frightened, angry child.

"Damn it, I don't understand!" he had shouted two years ago, the day the doctor broke the news. All this time, he had hoped it was just something minor, something that could be addressed by a pill or a dietary change—no more gluten or chocolate or dairy—something manageable. Carla had put out her hand as though to calm him, but he turned away.

"She's just thirty-five!" This to the doctor, as though age itself should have precluded the disease. He left the office, barely able to keep himself from slamming the door and blindly headed down the hall until he reached the men's room. Once inside, he locked the door, and then let the rage and fear and anguish pour out of him in a burning river of tears.

Carla never said a word about his reaction. Not when, red-eyed, he finally came back into the room. Not later that night when she was making a detailed list of everything she handled in their home and in their life—"just in case after surgery I'm not able to do it" she had said, but he knew what she was thinking: Just in case I die.

Not in the weeks and months that followed: before the operation and after, when radiation, attacking the remaining cancer cells, burned her insides as well, when chemo took away her hair, her appetite, her strength. Not when he would wake to find her sitting in the rocking chair by the living room window—the same chair where she used to rock Melodie to sleep during her bouts of colic—looking at the bare garden in the moonlight.

She had planted it the year she was pregnant with Melodie and had picked the first batch of tomatoes the day before she went into labor. Each year, she added something new. One year it was eggplant, another, a bed of asparagus. But last year she was too weak to work in the garden, and it had never occurred to him to do it for her, even though he knew how much she loved the sight of the young seedlings pushing their way through the fertile soil, a promise of the future.

One more way he had let her down.

But she never reproached him for failing her then or all the times after when he had not quite lived up to his own concept of what he should be: a strong man, a brave man, someone who would protect those whom he loved above all else.

He had failed Carla and now he had failed their daughter.

The car reached its apex and then began the slow, downward curve to the ground, and he tried again.

"There's the park by our house, Melodie," Adam said, forcing himself to release his grip on the bar and touching her shoulder to make her turn toward him, look at him, forgive him. Obediently, she turned her head to where he was pointing and smiled.

"I see it, Daddy," although he wasn't certain that she did. Maybe it was only a green blur, and she just wanted to give him that bit of success. Then it disappeared from view as the trees rose up to meet them before the ride began its ascent again, leaving behind the safety and security of solid ground.

"How many times will it go around?" He didn't realize he had asked the question aloud until Melodie answered.

"Three times, Daddy. This is just a baby ride," she emphasized. "When Mommy and I went to the state fair, we rode the big one—remember? That one went around five whole times and way faster than this one!"

He didn't remember. The three-hour drive to the fair and the almost twenty minutes it took to find a parking space and then the exorbitant admission price for the three of them— that's what he remembered. But the ride itself, watching the two of them circle like planets around the sun of the ride's center—*that* he didn't remember. He was too busy thinking about all the other long lines they would have to stand in before they could go back home. All the waiting, never sure that it was worth the time and effort.

"Sometimes it takes a few months before we can see any progress," the doctor had cautioned them. "We'll repeat the scan in twelve weeks, and then we'll know if we are on the right track."

It had been the longest three months of his life. He had felt like he was standing still even as the days passed. He just wanted it to be over, get the scan, know the results, and felt almost paralyzed in the meantime, unable to do anything, plan anything until he knew.

Not Carla, though. She marked off each day on the calendar and then went about her usual routine. She never even talked about it, although now he wondered if she had wanted to but knew that he didn't want to hear anything she might say, that he didn't want to be reminded that the outcome might not be the one they desired.

And when it did come, when the doctor came into the room holding the results, Adam didn't need to hear the words to know what they were. He could tell by the way the oncologist closed the file and set it on the desk and then paused before speaking. And in that moment, he felt himself falling, slipping through space and time with no one to stop him.

"Daddy, are you sleeping?" and this time Melodie gently laid her hand on his arm. "Open your eyes!"

Adam hadn't realized that he had shut them again, and embarrassed, he forced himself to look out. The maple leaves were beginning their annual change from green to reds and oranges and the cornfields that lined one side of the fairgrounds were giving up their plump ears to the combines slowly moving down the rows.

Carla loved the fall. No, that wasn't strictly true. Carla loved all the seasons: the fertile, wormy smell of spring when the rains softened the hard earth sufficiently for her to plant peas and lettuce, the hot and humid summer, when she alternately watered the garden and their daughter who ran squealing through the icy spray, and the fall when she brought the bright red tomatoes and long green peppers from the garden to their table.

And the winter—how she loved the winter. She would wait excitedly for the first snowfall, standing in the cold to allow the flakes to land on her hair, her coat, her upturned face. As soon as the outdoor rink was open, she would lace up her skates and carve ever-widening circles on the glassy surface, while he stood on the sidelines and watched.

Winter meant Christmas, and each year Carla started the holiday season in November, decorating their six-foot tree and every room in their home while the Thanksgiving turkey roasted in the oven.

"I think you still believe in Santa Claus," he had teased her the first year they were married, when she insisted that they go out in the sleet and icy wind on Christmas Eve to find him a stocking to hang. She still had hers from childhood, her name in glitter across the white fuzzy top, and was unwilling to let it be the only one adorning the non-working fireplace in their apartment.

"Of course I do," she said in mock shock, and smiled at him before grabbing his hand and running to a nearby drugstore where miraculously they found a red plush stocking with a white fuzzy top—a twin for hers. She grabbed it along with a small tube of glue and a packet of green glitter, and once back home, spelled out his name in beautiful cursive script.

He still had the stocking—hers, too. But last year he had left them as well as the carton of holiday decorations in the storage room. It didn't make sense to decorate, he told himself. They were spending Christmas Day at Susan's and then flying to Miami to spend the week in the sun.

"Won't that be fun?" he asked his daughter, but she only looked at him before going back to watch her television show. And as if to punish him, the Florida weather had been unseasonably overcast and damp, and Melodie caught a cold that left her irritable. Just last week, she asked if they were "going away again for Christmas," her tone resigned, not excited, and reluctantly he said they would stay home.

Melodie's face brightened for a moment but then she came closer to him and whispered, "But, Daddy, if you want to go to Florida again, that's okay, too," before leaving the room.

It was something Carla would have said. Was that what his daughter's role was now that her mother was gone—to be the one offering comfort?

He felt the gradual downward movement and the breeze, cooler now because evening was approaching. He glanced at his daughter, wondering if she was chilly, aware that he had forgotten to bring a sweater for her. One more in a long line of failures.

Adam wanted the ride to be over. He wanted to leave the fair, to go back home. There at least, he wouldn't have so many reminders of what he was supposed to have done, what Carla would have done, how many more times he would fail his daughter.

"Last time, Daddy," and Melodie moved closer to him as the car once again climbed into the sky. "If you want, we can go home when it's over," even though they hadn't bought the Belgian waffle she always ate or gone into the agricultural tents where home gardeners displayed their produce. Two years ago, Carla had won a blue ribbon for her sun, moon, and stars watermelon.

"Next year, I'll enter my zucchini," she had said, but that, like so many other things, didn't happen.

Did Melodie know what he was feeling? Was she, like her mother had, giving him an out?

"Okay, if you want to," putting the decision on her. It wouldn't be long now, he told himself. They would leave, he'd get her home, give her a snack, and tuck her in bed. And then—then what? Another long night drowsing in front of the television until, sometime after midnight, he stumbled up the hall to his empty bed?

A grinding noise broke into his thoughts and the wheel came to a halt, the mechanism no longer operational. Their car gently rocked at the top of the circle, suspended between heaven and earth. Around him, he could hear murmurs and a few frightened calls to the operator below, who was trying, as near as Adam could tell, to make the equipment start again.

Melodie shifted closer to him, trying to be brave, but he could see by her whitened face that she was frightened. This wasn't what was supposed to happen, she knew.

"What's wrong, Daddy?" she asked, her voice low and shaky. "Why did it stop?"

He took her hand, trying to be reassuring but more alarmed than he cared to admit, even to himself.

"It's okay," Adam said, but it wasn't. The ride wasn't supposed to stop. It was supposed to keep going until it came back down to earth, and it was their turn to get out of the metal car, stepping onto safe, familiar ground.

No, none of this was supposed to happen: not the broken Ferris wheel, not being a single parent, not burying his wife and trying to go on without her.

It wasn't supposed to happen, but it did, and no amount of fighting against the reality was going to change it.

"It's okay," he said again, and turned his daughter's face so she was looking at him, only him—not the ground so far away. "I'm with you and everything will be fine," and in that minute he even believed what he said, believed that he would be able to get them through this and everything else that lay ahead of the two of them. He might not do it as well as Carla would have done, or as well as the two of them together, but he would do his best.

He had to—because this was the way it was going to be.

There was a sudden jarring and then the ride began again, and the car descended until it reached the ground. Slowly, the Ferris wheel came to a halt and once the car had stopped swaying, the teenage operator leaned over, unlatched the bar, and said, "Okay, ride's over," adding perfunctorily, "Sorry for the delay."

Adam looked around him. They were right back where they had started—not surprising since the ride itself was stationary—yet somehow he felt as though they had stopped in a different place. Or was it he who had moved? Had the revolutions somehow transported him from the dark, grief-encased prison he had been in for almost a year to a light-filled, hope-filled room with windows and doors?

"Hurry up, Daddy!" Melodie simultaneously pulled at his arm and pushed his body with hers. She was anxious to get out, get moving, head to the next experience at the fair, and maybe too, the next experience in life. She was still young enough, despite the loss of her mother, to believe that good things awaited around the corner.

Unsteadily, Adam got to his feet, still feeling the swaying of the car in his body, then turned to take his daughter's hand.

"Come on, Melodie," he said. "Let's see what's ahead."

REMEMBER MAMA

"Maggie, where's my tea?"

Maggie set down the dishcloth and moved to answer her mother's call. The rest of the china, like so many other tasks half-completed, would have to wait.

"You had your tea already, Mama. Remember? I brought you a cup of tea and you finished it and said you didn't want any more."

But the old woman shook her head obstinately.

"No, I didn't. You never brought it. I've been waiting for hours" and the now-familiar note of self-pity crept into her voice, "and you never brought it to me."

Maggie smothered a sigh. There was no point in arguing with her mother. She could show her the cup she drank from and her mother still wouldn't remember.

Couldn't, Maggie corrected herself. Her mother couldn't remember. She had to keep reminding herself of that fact or the frustration would soon grow too strong to handle.

"Where is—where is—" Her mother struggled for a name and then gave up. "Where did he go?"

"Paul"—the name emphasized just a bit, "had to go away on a business trip. To California. I told you all about it, Mama. Remember?"

Paul—who had shown infinite patience and tenderness with his mother-in-law. He pretended everything was normal, and persisted in carrying on one-sided conversations with her about the weather, current events, upcoming plans for the weekend.

But lately, her mother couldn't even remember his name.

"Oh, yes, now I remember," but her mother's voice held no conviction. "It just slipped my mind for a moment," and she looked at her daughter, obviously hoping that the excuse would be accepted.

Maggie nodded her head, joining her mother in the delusion. "Mama's poor memory"—how often she and her father had teased her mother about her inability to recall names, dates, places. It had been humorous once, but no longer. Now it was a tragic reality.

After Maggie's father had died, her mother had become distracted and forgetful, and initially Maggie put much of the blame on grief. But even sorrow, she was finally forced to admit, couldn't wreak such havoc on a person's mental abilities. Even grief couldn't keep you from recalling where you lived, where you were going, whether or not you'd eaten or slept or changed your clothes. Only sickness could do that.

Remembering this, Maggie asked with more patience, "Do you want another cup of tea now, Mama?" as she straightened the soft throw across her mother's narrow, blue-veined feet. Maggie recalled watching her mother knit the soft mix of blue and cream and orchid yarns during the endless nights in the hospital, the sound of the long needles a counterpoint to the noise of the respirator that filled her father's lungs with air.

Someday, she would think, she would have to ask her mother to show her how to knit like that.

But there was never a free moment to learn. And now, her mother couldn't even tie her shoes.

"No, I'm not thirsty anymore. But I am hungry, Maggie. How soon is dinner?"

"Not for a long time, Mama. We just had lunch." Her mother frowned, and Maggie knew she didn't recall the omelet filled with cheese and herbs that her daughter had carefully prepared just half an hour ago. She went on quickly.

"I thought I'd make a roast for dinner, with new potatoes and green beans with dill. Would you like that for dinner, Mama?" knowing the question was pointless even as it was asked. No matter what her mother's initial response was, she was certain to change her mind by the time the food was ready. But Maggie had to keep the fiction alive that her mother's opinions and desires counted for something, as inconsistent as they were.

Her mother was silent for a moment, considering, and then shook her head. "I don't like beans—they've got strings. Why can't we have carrots instead?"

Maggie smiled. "Okay, Mama, I'll make carrots. Carrots in honey sauce, like you used to do. Why don't you take a little rest now while I finish washing the dishes?" and she stroked her mother's hair as the old woman obediently closed her eyes.

Slipping her fingers through the fine white strands, Maggie gazed with love and pity at her mother's face. With her eyes closed, her mother could be like any other old woman, just growing a bit more forgetful as years passed. Sometimes, Maggie could almost convince herself that this particular fantasy was real.

But then her mother would open her eyes to gaze blankly at her surroundings. The confusion that had been hidden behind those paper-thin lids would be painful to see, as Maggie watched her mother struggle to recall some recognizable pattern from the fading fabric of memory.

Suddenly, her mother moved her head, pulling it free from her daughter's caressing fingers.

"Leave me be," she said petulantly. "How can I sleep if you stand there bothering me?"

Maggie bit her lip, hurt by the sudden rejection.

"All right, Mama, I'll leave you alone. But call me if you need anything," and she slowly left her mother's side, returning to the kitchen where a pile of glasses and dishes waited to be washed and put away.

"Why did I decide to do this today?" she said aloud wearily, surveying the stack needing her attention. It was true the china closet was overdue for cleaning, but since her mother had come to stay, there was never enough time or energy for all those extra household chores.

Instead, there were endless trips to the grocery store, trying to keep abreast of her mother's strange and changeable food preferences. Visits to the doctor and drugstore, as medicines were tried, and, not surprisingly, failed to improve her mother's mental condition.

And there was finally the overwhelming and ever-present need to keep track of her mother—to watch where she was, what she was doing. And to keep her own temper in check, especially on those days when her mother would follow her from room to room, asking the same questions over and over until Maggie wanted to scream with frustration.

She plunged the dishes into the sudsy water one by one, and as the dust was washed away, the colors glowed in the light. Maggie wished, not for the first time, there was something she could give her mother to wash away this cruel disease and bring back the living colors and shades of her memory.

"But there's nothing I can do," she whispered hopelessly, rinsing the dishes and setting them to drain.

There were no pills, no medicine, nothing to turn this forgetful old woman into the vibrant mother she once had been. All Maggie could do was stand by and watch her mother's mind weaken a little more each day, while her body, in an ironic twist, remained relatively strong—a prison for the dying mind.

It's like a deathwatch, she thought. And I can't even reach her to say good-bye.

"What are you doing?" Her mother's voice startled Maggie, lost in her thoughts.

"Are you awake already, Mama? I was just finishing up the last of the dishes from the china cupboard. Do you remember this set?" and Maggie held up a bone china cup, rimmed with a delicate band of gold. "You used to tell me all about these when I was little. A wedding present to your grandmother. And these are the last two of the set."

The others had broken over the years. Old and delicate, too fragile to last during countless journeys through space and time.

And was that what happened to your mind, Mama? Maggie asked silently. Was it too fragile to take the strain of time as well?

Her mother glanced at the cup and then took it from Maggie's hand.

"What a pretty pattern," and Maggie couldn't tell from her voice if she was remembering or just commenting on a design she hadn't seen before.

"Yes, it is lovely," Maggie agreed and then reached for the cup. "But I have to put it away now, Mama."

But even as she moved to take it, her mother clutched it tighter in her thin hand, now almost as fragile and translucent as the cup itself.

"I'd like a cup of tea, Maggie," she said firmly. "I'm very thirsty and a cup would be nice right now. I think I'll make it myself" and she moved toward the stove. "I'll just brew a pot and pour it into this cup."

"I'd rather we used another one, Mama," Maggie said, trying to infuse her words with all the persuasion she could muster. "That cup is old—hot tea might shatter it."

She offered her mother a plastic mug, but the old woman shook her head.

"This cup, Maggie. I want this one. I never get to drink out of it anymore. And it used to be mine, you know," she added sharply. "I don't know why you are making such an issue."

Maggie sighed. Her mother was going to be difficult about the cup, as she had been lately about so many things. It wasn't that her mother cared what she drank from, Maggie knew. It was more as if she was testing Maggie's patience, trying to see how far she could push her daughter before she got angry.

It's like dealing with a two-year-old in a seventy-five-year-old body, Maggie thought. There was no reasoning with her at times like this. There was nothing she could do except wait until her mother's attention was captured by something else and Maggie could retrieve the cup, now held so carelessly in that bony hand.

She glanced at the stove and realized her mother had switched on the wrong burner, which was now beginning to heat, perilously close to her mother's outstretched fingers.

"Mama!" Maggie reached forward to pull her mother's hand away from the glowing element a fraction of a second before the skin could be burned. But her mother, startled by the sudden motion, released her hold on the cup and it shattered on the hardwood floor.

"I'm sorry, Maggie," her mother said worriedly, glancing up at her daughter, but Maggie shook her head.

"Let me see your hand, Mama," and she turned her toward the light, searching for blisters on the wrinkled skin. "Did you get hurt?"

"No, I'm fine. Really, Maggie. I didn't get hurt at all. I can't imagine how it happened," and she looked at the stove accusingly. "I'm sure I turned on the right burner. I didn't mean to break the cup," she added sadly, but Maggie only sighed, releasing her mother's hand.

"It doesn't matter, Mama," bending down to pick up the shattered fragments. "It was only a cup, after all. Why don't you sit down and I'll finish the tea."

"I don't think I want any after all, Maggie," her mother answered, sitting down at the small kitchen table. "You just go on with what you were doing and don't worry about me. I'll be fine," and she smiled anxiously at her daughter.

Maggie mustered a smile in response. It was almost as though her mother was afraid of her, afraid she'd roused her anger by breaking the cup.

But it was just an accident, Maggie told herself. Next time, I'll have to be more careful about letting Mama hold things.

And for a brief second, there flashed across her mind an endless succession of days spent keeping a closer and closer eye on her mother—watching her every move, trying to gauge her every thought—until the line blurred between mother and daughter and they merged into one.

"It doesn't matter," she repeated to herself and wasn't certain if she meant the cup or her ever-increasing responsibilities. It didn't matter. Maggie had to do it. This was her mother, after all.

"I'll just finish drying these dishes," she said aloud, "and then I'll start getting supper ready. Roast and potatoes and carrots, remember?" she added, before her mother could ask.

Her mother nodded her head. "Carrots in honey sauce," she said, surprising Maggie, who hadn't expected her to respond. "You said you'd do them like that for me. That's how I used to make them when you were little, Maggie. Lots of honey and butter," and she smiled, as though recalling a small child carefully spearing one golden ring after another, dripping with the sweet syrup.

Maggie held her breath. Her mother's lucid moments were rare and precious, for one never knew which one would be the last, which memory would be the final one snatched from the gathering mists.

But "I think I'd like a cup of tea now, Maggie," and the spell was broken, leaving Maggie to yearn for the other recollections of her childhood trapped inside her mother's mind.

She sighed. "I'll make it now, Mama. It will just take a moment," and the kitchen was silent, broken only by the sound of water heating in the kettle, and finally, the high thin sound of the whistle as the water reached the boiling point.

Maggie poured it into the waiting pot, and, as the tea steeped, dried the last few pieces of china. At least that job is done, she thought resignedly. It may have taken all day but now it can be crossed off the list.

The list itself seemed endless, with more items added than removed, especially in the last few weeks. Her mother's condition was a series of downward-turning spirals, with the deterioration increasing almost daily. It was as though her mother was gradually releasing her hold on reality, allowing her mind to drift farther away while Maggie watched helplessly from the shore, unable to bring her back.

"Here's your tea, Mama," and Maggie put the steaming cup on the table. "Watch, it's hot" and her mother paused to blow gently on the surface before taking a careful sip.

"It's good, Maggie," and Maggie relaxed and smiled.

"I'm glad, Mama," she answered warmly. "You finish it while I start supper. I'll get the carrots sliced," pulling them from the refrigerator, "and then you can tell me how to make the sauce."

She glanced at her mother as she set the scrubbed carrots in a pile on the table, hoping that the mention of the sauce would trigger another memory, another precious story of Maggie's childhood.

The older woman reached over to pull a carrot from the stack, and Maggie's heart leaped. She stopped slicing the golden spears and asked casually, "Do you want to help me, Mama?"

Her mother looked up at her. "Are these for dinner?"

"Yes, Mama." Maggie's smile began to fade but she determinedly kept her voice light. "I was going to clean them and then you would tell me how to make the sauce. With honey and butter. Remember?" unaware that a trace of desperation had crept into her voice. "Like you used to make for me, Mama, when I was little."

Her mother frowned. "I don't like carrots, Maggie. I like potatoes and spinach and maybe even celery—I don't know, I can't remember—" and her forehead crinkled in thought before smoothing out again. "But I know I don't like carrots."

Maggie was still, the carrot slices a tarnished heap before her.

"No, I don't like carrots—never did," her mother stated firmly. "How about green beans instead—nice fresh ones? What are we having for dinner, Maggie?"

LISTEN TO ME

"Listen to me. I want to tell you what happened today. On the bus. On the way to the doctor's. There was this girl, well, not a girl, she could have been about twenty-two or twenty-three, it's hard to tell these days, and she was wearing one of those things in her ears and she wasn't even watching the baby…"

His mother's voice followed Roger as he went into her kitchen. Hanging his jacket on the back of the kitchen chair, he turned his attention to the cabinets. The last time he was there, he noticed one of the doors hanging slightly askew. A loose screw—and he had made a mental note to bring his hand tools with him when he returned. Now, focused on fixing the problematic hinge, he heard her words in the background, the way you would hear someone talking when you're underwater. Muffled sounds, the consonants and vowels vaguely familiar but not quite the same as when your ears were above the surface. Something about a girl and a baby and a bus…

He finished tightening the screw, tested it a few times and then forced his awareness through her tide of words until he got to the shore—the beginning of it all, the part following her opening dive into the conversation: "Listen to me."

"I don't care about the girl," coming back into the living room. But even to Roger, the interruption sounded far too abrupt, hostile even. So he tried again, more gently. "What about the doctor? What did he say?"

His mother stopped talking and turned away, her fingers folding the newspaper with unnecessary care and attention. She wished he wouldn't keep bringing that up. "Nothing. I mean, nothing new. Just keep taking the pills and he'll see me again in a month. Waste of money, I think, and time, too. So anyway, the baby was sucking on the seatback and it was so dirty—the seat, not the baby—and I wanted to say something, but you know how young people are these days, so I just looked away because, really what could I do?"

"No tests? No bloodwork?" rooting through the store bag he had set on the end table until he found the batteries. It was fall, time to replace them in the combination smoke and carbon monoxide detector just outside her bedroom door. Or maybe he should buy a new one, one of those that not only sent out a warning signal but had flashing lights and verbal announcements as well: "Fire! Fire!" "Carbon monoxide detected!" "Danger! Danger!" "Exit now!" She'd be safer then, as long as she listened to the warning and obeyed the directions.

She nodded. "Well, they always do that" as though he ought to know the procedure. And he should. There was a time when he accompanied her on the visits, meticulously recorded the doctor's comments, lab results, orders for more tests, more treatment. But then, little by little, she started going without him. Or was he the one who had stopped accompanying her?

Whose decision was it, or was it an unspoken agreement between the two of them?

"So, Roger—listen to me" and there it was again, the demand for him to pull his attention from what really mattered, the line of thought he was pursuing, the maintenance chores he was completing, to follow her down a tributary of little interest to him but apparently of major importance to her. "When I was getting off at the corner of Twentieth and Pacifica, I said to her, 'There are so many germs on buses' but she never even looked up at me. I don't know. Maybe she didn't hear me or she didn't care," and she set the newspaper on the end table, so he could take it to the recycling bin. "Even if she had heard me, I don't know that it would have mattered."

"So when do you go back?" and Roger pulled out his phone to record the date and time. He would go with her. After all, he needed to know what was happening. He needed to hear the words—directly from the doctor, not lost in the waves of her segues and irrelevancies—that would tell him what to expect.

"I don't know. They said they would call and set it up because I forgot to bring my datebook with me and I didn't want to take just any appointment in case I already had something scheduled."

Not that there was anything she had to consider. Little by little, she watched as her wall calendar became emptier, with more bare blocks than filled. The weekly hair appointment— no longer needed, since even her arthritic fingers could easily wash the cottony baby fuzz. The Monday and Thursday bingo also cancelled—Roger worried that, with the chemo, there was too great a risk of catching germs. And church—it had been a long time since she had been inside St. Matthew's. Instead, she watched the religion channel on TV, sometimes reciting the prayers, but more often than not, dozing through the hour-long service, not waking until the final benediction was offered.

Her priest said that counted just as if she had come to Mass, although she didn't tell him about the sleeping part. Maybe he was right. Or maybe she should have told him. But he was in a hurry that day—usually the deacon came to the apartment but this time it was Father Mike himself—and she wasn't sure he had enough time for a conversation, to actually listen to her.

"I'll call them and let you know," he said, adding a note to his already jammed calendar. Despite his best intentions, a tiny sigh escaped his lips.

But she heard it and shook her head. "No, I'll do it. I don't want to be a bother. If I had known you were coming by, I would have called them already. And look, I'll do it now"—and she reached for the phone only to stop. "No, it's noon. They'll be at lunch and not taking calls. I'll call later and let you know," and she smiled at him as though it was all settled and he had nothing to worry about.

And it was, at least to her way of thinking. There were things he could fix and things that he couldn't. He was a good son, her Roger. He always had been. She should tell him that now. But if she did—if she shifted the conversation from day-to-day events to something more personal—he would start asking questions she didn't want to answer.

She plucked at the corner of her lap robe, pulling it higher. Even though she kept the apartment at 78 degrees, she still felt chilled.

Roger put away his phone and went to help her, noticing the bruises like purple puddles on her right forearm. There were more of them this week, he noted, giving the appearance of a badly done tattoo sleeve. Yes, he had better go next time, bring it to their attention. Maybe there was something they could do—start a pill or stop one. Maybe there was something that was reflected in her lab tests that they had overlooked. She trusted the doctor, but he didn't—not really. After all, she was just an old woman to them, a patient on her way out the door. Why waste those precious appointment minutes with her when there were those so much younger who needed the time—who had, in theory at least, more time?

But he'd make them answer his questions. He'd make them listen to him. She wasn't just an old woman. She was his mother.

Roger tucked the blanket around her shoulders, then, retrieving the stepladder from the closet, he replaced the burned-out bulb in the hallway and put the fresh batteries in the smoke detector. Two more items on his list to check off, but he wondered how many more needed to be done. She never let him know when things weren't working. He had to find out for himself.

"Ma," he had said just last week, when he realized the shut-off valve for the toilet was leaking, "you have to tell me when things aren't working right! Otherwise, I won't know! And if I don't know, I can't fix them!"

But she had just waved at him as though it wasn't important, didn't matter, and handed him a cookie she had made, asking, "Do you think it's too dry?"

He had said it was fine, although it stuck in his throat. Or maybe it wasn't the cookie but all those worries: about those broken items, those damaged pieces, those failing parts that he wanted to repair but deep down inside was afraid that he couldn't.

The week's tasks done, he came back into the living room. "And the results? Did they give you the printout like I asked you to get?"

She was happy to see her son but wished he didn't focus so much on her health or the doctor visits or the results. Ever since he was a little boy, Roger wanted to fix things, make them work better. She still remembered the toolbox he got for his sixth birthday, and how he ran around the apartment looking for broken items that he could repair. That's what he did in his job—fix things—but here there was nothing for him to work on.

Not now.

Not anymore.

So instead of answering, she got up from the recliner—the one he had bought his father the year before he died—and went into the bathroom. And when she returned, it was to start a new conversation, as though the last question had been asked and answered.

"So, Roger, you know Mrs. Abernathy across the way, the one whose cat was hit by a car last month? So, her daughter-in-law bought her a tiny dog and she named it Bella and she came over here with it and—listen to me, Roger, don't go through that stack!" and he turned from the pile of prescription bags and unopened envelopes from Medicare and the bank.

"I'll take these with me and go over them, okay?" but she frowned.

"I can do it. Leave them there. So, the dog, Bella, she laid on my lap so quiet and just wagged her tail and—listen to me! I told you to leave them!" her voice surprisingly firm and insistent, the way it was when he was a child and didn't obey her the first time. "Come here and listen to me!"

Frustrated, Roger set the paperwork and envelopes back down on the table and came over, stooping down in front of her. And that was when he noticed the glint of tears in her eyes.

"Just listen to me," she repeated, and he caught the undercurrent of pleading, as though all she wanted was for him to stop asking questions, stop doing tasks—stop everything and just listen to her.

Roger took her cold hands in his. "I'm sorry, Ma. Talk to me. I'm listening."

NEW LOVERS, OLD LOVERS

HENRY, HORTENSE AND THE HALLOWEEN PARTY

"Hi, Henry! I'm home."

No answer.

The apartment was quiet. Too quiet. Ominously quiet.

It was clear that Henry was still sulking.

It all began a few weeks ago when I had decided to host a Halloween party. Deep in party-planning mode, I had already made a list of what to serve (my signature devil's brew chili with pitchers of Bloody Marys to wash it down) and how to decorate (lots of black candles and illuminated jack-o-lanterns). And to set the mood, I decided to rent a few black-and-white horror movies from the local library.

I was online scrolling through the list to find just the right ones when Henry drifted into the living room. That's when it all started.

"*The Evil Ghost of Dublin Grange. The Phantom of the Bookshop. The Spectre in Solloway Castle*," he said, reading aloud the titles I had checked. Then he looked at me accusingly. "I thought we had a deal, Jennifer."

I sighed. I had known it would come to this. Ever since I started talking about having a Halloween party, I knew I was treading on thin ice as far as Henry was concerned. He didn't care what I did for Christmas, Valentine's Day, or the Fourth of July. But when it came to Halloween, Henry had very firm opinions about what was not appropriate—and they all centered around any depictions of ghosts, spirits, or other forms of apparitions as evil, malevolent, or even slightly malicious, which pretty much ruled out every representation of otherworldly bodies.

"How would you feel if I had a party and the movies I chose were all about single women who hated their jobs and had no love life and ended up attacking innocent people?" he demanded when I first brought up the subject a few months ago, just after I had moved into the apartment.

I had allowed that he might have a point—not that I really thought he had one—and dropped the subject, hoping that by the time October rolled around, he would change his mind. After all, we didn't know each other all that well yet, and I recognized that adjustments would have to be made. That's what everyone went through when they had roommates.

And when it came to people like Henry, my experience was pretty limited, which is to say, non-existent. In principle, I liked his type, or at least, the concept of his type. And on the whole, Henry was a lot easier to deal with than some of the other roommates I had lived with. He didn't hog the bathroom, eat my food, or take over the television remote. He stayed to his area, wherever that was since I didn't know where he spent his time when he wasn't around me. In short, Henry was fairly accommodating.

So, as I said, I let it go and bided my time. But I wasn't willing to give up the idea because I really wanted a Halloween party. I loved the whole concept of Halloween: the scary costumes, the spooky sound effects, the spine-tingling possibility that somewhere out there might just be an actual evil spirit waiting to catch you unawares. I had never outgrown the Ouija board-and-séance stage of my youth, as evidenced by my preference for goth décor and my ever-growing collection of books dealing with spiritualism, ghosts, and the afterlife—all courtesy of the local metaphysical bookstore, Books and Bones.

It was my choice of reading material that initially drew us together. I was in the middle of unpacking my books when Henry first appeared, and, after introducing himself with a simple, "Hello, Jennifer, I'm Henry," he came over to inspect my personal library.

"I can see that you appreciate the spiritual realm. That's important to me," giving me an approving look.

"Well, I like to think that spirits are people too," I said—not the most original line I could have come up with, but it was the best I could do under the circumstances. After all, I wasn't expecting to find my apartment came with a roommate, especially one like Henry.

But I was open-minded, and as it turned out, Henry was good company. He was there when I awoke and there when I came home from work, always willing to listen to me complain about my bosses or my lack of social life.

Sometimes we'd spend our evenings debating the relative merits of séances versus crystal balls as a way to summon the dead or discussing how spirits were portrayed in literature. We talked about our favorite authors, with Henry favoring Mary Shelley and Edgar Allan Poe—not surprising since he was of that era, after all—while I leaned toward twentieth-century authors, like Stephen King, Shirley Jackson, and Daphne du Maurier.

Despite the obvious differences in our ages and physical (or in Henry's case, metaphysical) appearances, we had more in common than a lot of other couples I knew. Except when it came to our views on the October holiday.

There the divergence was Grand Canyon in size, and I didn't know how to bridge it. So, I took the same approach I had used (albeit unsuccessfully) when I had encountered problems in my other relationships: I ignored it. And when October came around, I went ahead with my party plans, hoping Henry's objections had faded away.

But they hadn't, which was evident when he saw the list of movies I was reserving.

"A deal's a deal, Jennifer," he said flatly.

"But damn it, Henry, this is my apartment, too! I pay the rent and the utilities! I should be able to have a party if I want to! Why do you have to be so difficult?"

"Difficult?" he shot back. "You don't know how difficult I could be! I could make your life pretty miserable if I wanted to! I could bang on walls or turn lights off and on! And what would you say to your landlord if you tried to break your lease—that the place was haunted? He wouldn't buy that excuse and you'd be out your deposit and the rent money! And you'd have to find a new place to live! You ought to just be grateful and give in on this one little thing!" and then he disappeared.

"Henry, come back," I said in my best wheedling tone. But there was no response. "Come on, Henry, I know you're there. Look, if I only get one movie, will that be okay? After all, I'm not responsible for Hollywood's views on goblins, you know!"

"A ghost is not the same as a goblin. How many times do I have to explain that to you? A ghost is the spirit of a person, but a goblin was never human to begin with."

I twisted around in my chair and there he was again, with that "I'm still angry" look on his face. I grinned. "I love it when you talk didactic to me."

But Henry wasn't ready to forgive me. He gave me one final look and then stomped out of the room (if a ghost could be said to stomp), leaving behind a definite chill in the air.

His absence continued for the rest of that evening, and for the days that followed. Each afternoon when I came home from work and called out, "Hi, Henry, I'm home!" there was no return "Hi, Jennifer! How was your day?" response to greet me.

Worse, there was no one I could discuss our relationship problem with, since I had kept Henry out of my conversations with my friends. It wasn't like I could casually say, "By the way, I'm having a little difficulty with my roommate Henry. He's a little older than me, well a lot older—about a century or so—and he is really opposed to me having a Halloween party. Any advice?"

While my friends were generally open-minded, even they might draw the line at my belief that my apartment was haunted. And it wasn't like I could count on Henry to appear on command and demonstrate that he wasn't a figment of my imagination but was instead a real-life apparition—if that wasn't a contradiction in terms.

No, I couldn't get anybody's help on how to handle this issue, and the longer it went on, the worse I felt. We were at a stalemate, and as Henry's absence continued, I didn't know how to break it. He had vanished—from my sight and apparently from the apartment as well, since I didn't have that "Henry's home" sensation: the very slight tingling you get when you think there's someone watching you. No, like Elvis, Henry had "left the building" and I didn't know how to convince him to return.

So here I was, with the party just two weeks away, and I was no closer to resolving the problem. If I cancelled the event, my friends would be disappointed. But if I had the party, Henry would be angry, and might return just in time to make his feelings known to everyone in attendance. It was a no-win situation.

And to make it worse, I had high hopes for this party. It would be the first one I was holding since my last love affair ended (hence the change in my living location), and I had encouraged my girlfriends to bring a few unattached guys. While Henry was lots of fun to hang out with, there were indisputable limitations to our relationship. Granted, we could go to a movie together, but dining out would definitely raise some eyebrows, unless I wanted the other patrons to see me apparently talking to myself. And once we got back to my apartment—well, there was only so much one could do when the other person lacked a solid presence.

The Halloween party would hopefully resolve that issue if a suitable male showed up. And if Henry behaved himself and didn't cause any trouble.

But the fact was that the longer this went on, the more I realized that I missed Henry. Weird as it may sound, the two of us had developed a true friendship and I wasn't sure if the party was worth ruining it. What could I do to mend the fence that was clearly broken? What should I say to him the next time I saw him? For that matter, how could I find him to say whatever it was that I wanted to, since he was choosing to remain absent?

By the Thursday before the party, I was ready to say or do anything to let Henry know that I was sorry I hadn't taken his feelings into account. First, I walked around my apartment, calling to him like he was a house pet: "Here, Henry, where are you? Come on, Henry, come to Jennifer!" But no response was forthcoming.

Then I tried apologizing: "Henry, you were right, and I was wrong and please forgive me." But still no reaction.

I even tried pleading: "Henry, please come back. I won't ever have a Halloween party again! I promise!" But Henry remained stubbornly AWOL.

It was well past midnight and I had just crawled into bed when I felt that old familiar chill, but stronger than it had ever been before. And suddenly there was Henry, standing in my bedroom doorway.

"Oh, Henry, you're back!" I pushed back the covers, intending to go to him but paused when he made a weird jerking move, as though someone had pushed him from behind. And then I saw her, a lovely red-haired girl wearing a long lace gown and bonnet—and a very determined look on her face.

"Go on, Henry," and she gave him another firm shove. "Say it!"

Henry sighed and then, looking down at the floor, recited what was evidently a practiced statement. "I'm sorry for being so angry with you, Jennifer. You have every right to enjoy your holiday."

"And," prompted the girl, and he sighed again.

"Please forgive me."

"Oh, Henry, of course I forgive you and I'm so glad you're back!" I started to rush over to him but then stopped short. After all, it wasn't as if I could give him a hug. So, I settled for adding, "I've missed you, Henry" hoping he could hear the sincerity in my voice.

He looked up at me, and I could see it was that old familiar Henry again. "I missed you, too, Jennifer," and he smiled.

"Henry?" the girl said, and he turned around.

"Oh, I'm sorry, my dear. Let me introduce you. Jennifer, this is Hortense. Hortense, this is Jennifer. We met two weeks ago when I was, when I was…" and he stopped, apparently not sure what to say next.

"When you were being such a stick-in-the-mud about Jennifer's party plans," said Hortense with a smile. "My goodness, I have never seen anyone so angry! He came up to the fifth floor—that's where I live—and he was stomping around on the landing, making so much noise I had to finally come out and tell him to stop! If he had kept that up, he was likely to make my roommate Peter want to move out. So, I gave him what-for and—"

"And I was so taken by her beauty that I couldn't say anything more than I was sorry," he finished, with an expression on his face that I had never seen before. "And when I tried to explain why I was so angry—"

"I told him that he was being a ninny and that he was lucky to have you as a roommate and that he had to apologize," Hortense interjected. "And eventually he agreed."

Judging by the look she gave him, I suspected that she had worn him down until he had no choice—a neat trick and one that I should learn how to do. It would come in handy in my relationships.

"So here we are," she finished. "And besides, he owes you a thank-you, too."

"For what?" I asked and I thought I could see a faint blush on Henry's cheeks.

"For the two of us meeting," Hortense explained. "If he hadn't been so angry, he wouldn't have left your apartment and come upstairs. Then we wouldn't have gotten to know each other. Isn't that right, Henry?" and he nodded, a sheepish look on his face.

"And it turns out that Hortense and I have a lot in common—even more than *we* do, Jennifer! Not that I don't value our friendship," he added hastily, apparently worried that I might take offense and he'd be in hot water with me and his new love interest. "But you know, Jennifer, there are just some things that only another spirit can understand."

"Of course, Henry, and I'm very glad you found someone," although it was a little irritating that while I had successfully, albeit unknowingly, played Cupid for a ghost, I couldn't find a living breathing love interest for myself. And judging by that sappy smile on his face, he would most likely be spending every minute with her, doing whatever two spirits in love do and leaving me all by myself.

Hortense's next words indicated that she sensed what I was thinking. "You know, Jennifer, you should meet Peter. You two have a lot in common. You're about the same age, you're both unattached and—"

"And you both believe in ghosts," said Henry. "That's what ended his last relationship, right, Hortense?" and she nodded.

"That's true. All he did was mention to her that he had a roommate, and then, when he explained who I was—or, more accurately, what I was—she told him that he was crazy and it was over."

"She was so conventional," Henry added. "Not at all like you" and I smiled at the praise.

"I just know you and Peter would get along. Why don't you ask him to your party?" Hortense suggested.

But I shook my head. "I just think it would be weird to invite someone I don't know and who doesn't know me to a party at my place, even if we do live in the same building. I mean, we haven't even met!"

"That's true," she said thoughtfully. "It's too bad…" She paused then grabbed Henry's hand. "My goodness, it's late! Jennifer, you need to get some sleep! Come on, Henry!"

And before I could even say goodbye, the two of them vanished from sight, leaving me wondering if I had dreamed the entire encounter.

The next afternoon I stopped by Books and Bones on my way home to pick up some new reading material, since it looked like Henry would be spending a good portion of his evenings with his new ladylove. Once back at the apartment building, I was trying to hold my purchases with one hand while I struggled to pull my keys from my pocket with the other, when someone bumped into me, sending my stack of books flying.

"Damn it! Can't you watch where you're going?" I turned to my assailant and found myself staring directly into the sexiest pair of blue eyes this side of Paul Newman.

"I'm so sorry! I don't know what happened!" the man said, bending down to pick up my books. "I saw you there and was going to unlock the door for you—I live here, too—when suddenly it was like I was pushed from behind. I guess I tripped or something," he added.

"No, really, it's okay," and I reached for my books, not wanting him to see the titles. But it was too late. He had already noticed them.

"This is a really great book on the rise of spiritualism in popular culture." He handed it over and then collected the rest from the sidewalk. "Of course, it's not as detailed as Professor Harriet Allgood's work"—a name I was familiar with since I owned at least three of her books—"but it does give a different perspective on the reasons for the growing interest."

I didn't know what to say. Could I actually have met an attractive man who shared my affinity for all things metaphysical?

"Um, yes, well, I just picked it up at—"

"Books and Bones, right?" he finished. "That's the only place I know of that carries these types of books. I'm there at least once a month myself. Funny we never met."

"Yeah, funny," I answered, not knowing what else to say.

"Here, let me unlock the door," and once inside, he said, "If it's okay, I'll give you a hand getting all these to your apartment. What floor are you on? Oh, and I guess I should introduce myself. My name's Peter."

Peter. Of course. Who else could it be?

"I'm Jennifer. Third floor," I added and the two of us climbed the stairs. The whole way up, I felt like I was being watched, and when we reached my apartment, I knew why. There was Henry and next to him, Hortense, the two of them looking far too pleased with themselves. I remembered what Peter said, something about being pushed from behind, and I knew who was responsible.

"Henry?" and at the same time Peter said, "Hortense?"

"We just thought you two should meet, since you both have a shared interest," said Hortense innocently. "You have told him about the party, haven't you, Jennifer?"

Peter looked at me and I could feel my cheeks redden. "Well, actually, I'm having a little Halloween get-together tomorrow night, nothing real big, just a few friends and—"

"And she would love to have you come," said Henry, since I was obviously having difficulty finishing my sentence.

"Of course!" he responded immediately. "What can I bring? Food? Drinks? Oh, I know!" and he looked at Hortense. "Remember that CD I bought last year, the one with bloodcurdling screams and howling noises and gusty winds? That would be just the thing to set the mood!"

Hortense nodded. "Absolutely! So, Jennifer, we'll see you tomorrow—seven o'clock, right?" and then she looked at Henry. "Right, Henry?"

"Yes, dear," he said, nodding reluctantly.

So that was how it came to be that my Halloween party expanded to include three more guests. Henry and Hortense spent most of the evening out on the tiny balcony off the living room, with Hortense keeping Henry too occupied for him to engage in any ghostly behaviors that might give the others in attendance pause. As for Peter—well, sufficient to say that the attention he paid to me made it clear that Hortense's suggestion had been a good one.

"That was a great party, Jennifer," said Peter, coming up to me after the last guest had left. "Thanks for inviting me."

"Well, thanks for coming," sounding for all the world like a prim and proper hostess. But I guess it didn't matter because Peter leaned forward and gave me the kind of kiss that made words superfluous. I don't know if it was his idea or if Hortense had given him a nudge, but in the end, it didn't matter.

"Yes, I do think the party was a great success," said Hortense with a sly smile once I came up for air. "I think we should do this every year! Don't you think so, Henry?"

Henry looked at the two of us and then at Hortense and surrendered to the inevitable. "Yes, dear."

WITH ANY LUCK

"This can't be happening."

Amy looked at the basement floor in disbelief. It was wet. Very wet. Sopping, in fact. There was water at the base of the steps and under the pile of boxes where the movers had set them at her instructions. The boxes she had yet to sort through.

The water tank was undeniably leaking. That was bad enough but what made it worse was that there was no valve at the top to stop the cold water from flowing into the tank and back out again through the crack at the bottom. And that was complicated by the reality that it was eleven at night and she was alone in a house she had just moved into that morning, in a small town where the only person she knew was Sheila Jones, the real estate agent who had handled the sale.

"Damn it damn it damn it," her words coming nearly as fast as the stream of water. "Now what am I supposed to do?"

She was tired. She was dirty. All she wanted was to take a hot shower and go to bed and try to put the events of the past two years behind her. Instead, she had to find the main water valve and turn it off, which would not only stop the water from going to the tank, but also to every other plumbing-related fixture in the house: the kitchen sink, the toilet, the bathtub.

It was a very bad ending to a very long day.

"I thought I paid to have the house inspected!" were her first words to Sheila the next morning, barely allowing the woman to finish her "Thank you for calling All the Best Realty. How may I help you?" greeting. "Why wasn't this caught? Instead, I had to go to bed without showering, and since there was no water, I couldn't even make my coffee this morning! And I had to brush my teeth using ginger ale!"

And the memory of that unpleasant ginger-peppermint combination was almost enough to make her throw up.

"But Amy, the home inspector did point out that the water tank was old and that you should consider having it replaced," said Sheila, her reasonable tone doing nothing to calm Amy down.

"Okay, okay, but what am I supposed to do now? I need it fixed right away!"

"I'll call Eddie, our local handyman, and ask him if he can come over, take a look at it, and see what he recommends," she answered. "He does all kinds of work—plumbing, electrical, roofing—and he's very reliable. Will you be home all morning?"

"Well, yeah, since I can hardly go anywhere until I get cleaned up!" Amy paused. "I'm sorry. I don't mean to snap. I'm just—"

"Don't worry about it. Let me call him right now, and I'll have him text you when he can get there. And I'll check in with you later to see how it's going, okay?"

"Well, it will have to be, I guess," answered Amy, as she worried what kind of hit this would take to her already depleted finances. "Thanks, Sheila," trying for an appreciative tone but failing.

While she waited for Eddie's text, Amy looked through the folder holding all the purchase documents until she found the inspection report. She read through it and saw the notation, even highlighted in bright yellow: "Water tank is more than thirty years old. Buyer should consider replacement."

Sheila was right. But it didn't help. As a matter of fact, it only made things worse, pointing out one more instance where her failure to identify a warning sign and take action to address it resulted in a catastrophe.

Like not asking her now ex-husband where the extra money had come from for the sports car he bought three years ago. Like not accompanying him to the accountant's office when it came time to do their joint taxes, but instead just signing her name on the line of the return. Like not wondering why he decided to have their mail go to a post office box instead of having it delivered right to their home.

And by the time Matt was arrested, charged with embezzlement, and ultimately convicted, it was too late to ask questions or prepare for the inevitable financial fallout. Instead, all she could do was sell their condo and leave town as quickly as possible, more ashamed than her ex about what had happened.

That's how she ended up in Eden, a small rural village where housing prices were more in line with her suddenly straitened circumstances. The thousand-square-foot cottage was priced within her means, she had thought, never considering that all those maintenance expenses once handled by the condo management would now fall on her—including a failed water tank.

The alert tone sounded on her phone, interrupting her thoughts. It was a text message: "This is Eddie, Sheila's handyman. She said you need help. I'm right around the corner, so I'm on my way. OK?"

Okay? No, it's not okay, thought Amy. I'm still in my robe and pajamas!

But what option did she have?

"OK," she texted back and went out to the front porch where she kicked away the fallen leaves from the doorway. Another job she would have to handle, which meant she'd need to buy a rake and trash bags and…

But before her mind could finish adding the latest chore to her new homeowner To-Do list, a blue pickup with rusted fenders pulled into her drive. Sheila hadn't said what this handyman looked like, but when Eddie got out of the driver's side, he certainly wasn't what she expected. He looked more like a hardcore biker, wearing a baseball cap and jean jacket, both emblazoned with motorcycle logos. And when he removed his jacket, tossed it onto the front seat, and came closer, she could see that his forearms were covered with tattoos: a combination of flowers, an American flag, and a motorcycle outlined in red and black.

Instinctively, she tightened the belt of her robe and then shoved her hands in the pockets. What kind of man had Sheila sent? she thought, but did her best to hide her discomfort as he came onto the porch.

"Eddie," he said, holding out his hand, but when she didn't respond, he gave her a quizzical look from his brown eyes, half-hidden under the brim of his cap.

She flushed, gave him a quick handshake, and then led him inside. "I don't know what happened—well, I do know, that is. The water tank is leaking, but I don't know why. Except that it's old. That's what the inspector said. And I was going to replace it, but I didn't have the money and—"

She stopped then, realizing that her unease was making her chatter like a monkey, and took a deep breath. "I'm sorry. It's just that…" stopped again, and then continued. "I'm Amy. Amy Allison. I just moved in yesterday, and when I went downstairs last night, I saw water all over the floor. And the water tank doesn't have a shutoff, so I had to turn off the main. Which meant I couldn't even take a shower!"

She stopped again, wondering why she had added that last bit and if he could tell by her appearance and possibly smell that it was at least twenty-four hours since she'd bathed. But Eddie just stood there, patiently waiting.

Flushing, she gestured toward the hallway. "The door to the basement is in the kitchen," and she let him go ahead of her, deciding to wait upstairs.

In less than ten minutes Eddie was back in the kitchen. "You need a new water heater. And two shutoffs: one each for the hot and cold supply lines. There's a hardware store in town that'll have everything I need. Let's go so you can pick out the size you want and pay for everything. Then all you'll owe me is my time."

Amy looked at him in disbelief. Go to the store with him the way she looked? Was he nuts?

"I can't go anywhere until I've had a shower," she said firmly, and heard a tiny exhalation escape from his lips.

"Then how about this? I'll call them and get the prices and sizes, and you can give them your credit card number. I'll go get it and come back and install it. And then," he added, with a slight grin, "you can get yourself cleaned up."

"Fine, fine," she muttered ungraciously. But why was she taking it out on him? It wasn't his fault the tank was leaking. Or Sheila's. Or the fault of the home inspector, for that matter. It was all Matt's fault.

And mine, too, for not paying attention, she thought, as she dug through her wallet for the one credit card that wasn't yet maxed out. In the background, she heard Eddie on his phone detailing what he would need and checking prices.

"Ms. Allison?" and she turned. "Do you want a thirty-gallon or a forty-gallon tank?"

"I don't know," she said helplessly. The condo association had put in whatever was needed and neither she nor Matt had ever had to replace it.

"Hmm… If it's just you, a forty-gallon should be plenty. You can go with a thirty-gallon, but they actually cost more."

"Fine, then forty it is," she said and stood there, card in hand as she waited for the final figure.

Eddie went back to his phone to report her choice, then asked for the total. "Hold on a minute, Bobby," he said and looked at the notes he scribbled down before reading them off to her. "The tank will run you $500, plus two supply line connectors at $40 each for a total of $580. Plus, the sales tax which brings it to a grand total of $613.35." He looked at her, waited a second, then added, "The gas supply line looks solid so that will save you some money, at least."

Thank God, she thought, taking his phone so she could give the clerk her card information, and then handed it back so he could finish the call.

"I'll be back in about an hour with everything, and then it will take me at least an hour to get it in place. So, the good news is—" And is there good news? she wondered—"you should be back in business by this afternoon."

He waited a moment and then said, "Okay, then, I'll see you about eleven," but when Amy just nodded, he shrugged his shoulders and went out the front door, leaving it open.

Once she heard his truck pull out, Amy shut and locked the door. She had been rude to him. She knew that. She should have thanked him for getting this done so quickly. She knew that, too. But she wasn't exactly in a thankful state of mind.

#

Eddie got into the truck, debated briefly about going back to shut the front door. The hell with it, he decided, reversing down the driveway. He had rearranged his schedule on the fly, putting off the calls he was supposed to make first thing this morning, and she couldn't even bother to say thanks. And now he'd have to work even later than his usual 7 p.m. quitting time. By the time he reached the store, his irritation had mounted.

"What's her problem, anyway?" he asked when he called Sheila to give her an update. "It's not my fault she has a bad water tank!"

"I know, I know," Sheila said soothingly. "I got an earful when she called me. But try to understand. The move has been very stressful for her. The divorce was difficult enough, plus there were circumstances—well, that's really her business—but anyway that's why she left the city and came here. She just wanted to get away from the situation and all the embarrassment around it."

Sheila paused, and Eddie waited to hear if she was going to tell him more, but instead, she just went on. "To make matters worse, her ex left her with a mound of bills so now she's got to find a job. I guess the water tank was the last straw," adding with a laugh, "She might have been in a better mood if she'd at least had her coffee!"

Eddie grinned, taking a swig from his thermos. He never left his place without filling it to the brim with his fully leaded beverage. "I can understand that! All right, I'll cut her some slack. I'll text you when I'm done over there, but in the meantime, can you call the next two people on the list and explain that I'm running behind? Gotta go."

After loading up his truck with Amy's order, he started back to her house. Then, remembering what Sheila had said, he detoured to Joe's Joint to pick up a coffee and doughnut.

"That might improve her mood," he said, downing another swallow from his thermos. He cranked up the radio to hear his favorite country music, hoping it might ease some of his own tension, although why he felt that way, he wasn't sure. He'd had grouchy customers before. What was it about this one that got under his skin? But by the time he reached Amy's house, the combination of caffeine and Johnny Cash had done the trick, and he was in a better frame of mind. He'd do the job, take his money, and that would be that.

"Here," he said, thrusting the coffee and bag with the doughnut at her, when she opened the door. "Sheila said you missed your morning cup of joe."

"Um, thanks," setting it on the side table. "But did you get the tank?"

"Yes," with heavy patience. "Hold the door open, and I'll get it in and get started."

As he loaded the cardboard box encasing the tank onto the dolly, Eddie was barely able to restrain himself from shaking his head. Not even a thank you, he thought. Okay, she had problems. So what? Everybody has problems, thinking of old lady Carlson who needed a handicap ramp at her house before she was released from the hospital—one of the jobs that was on his list for today. A job that should have been done already except that he was here instead.

I'll get this done and then I'm out of here, he told himself. One hour. That's all it should take.

Unfortunately, nothing went as smoothly as Eddie had hoped. While he was able to wheel the hundred-pound tank up the porch stairs, down the hallway, and into the kitchen, dealing with the basement doorway presented another issue. It was too narrow to accommodate the box, and he was forced to remove the door and surrounding frame so he could get the unit through the opening and down the basement steps. The old tank was harder to disconnect than he had expected and even harder to manhandle up the narrow stairs. Then, when he went to open the shutoff to the house's supply line, it broke, and he had to dig through his parts box to find another to replace it.

All the while, Amy watched him, not that she had any idea what he was doing, he thought. And he had no intention of explaining. He just wanted to get the job done and leave.

Finally, after two hours of frustration and setbacks, Eddie was finished. He carried his tools upstairs, and then stopped at the kitchen table to write up his invoice.

"That'll be $70—$35 an hour," he said, handing her the bill.

Amy looked at it and then back at him, an expression of disbelief on her face. "But you said it would only take one hour!"

"I said at *least* an hour," Eddie reminded her. "Look, I didn't even charge you for the extra valve I had to install at the main! And if I were you, I'd add shutoffs at a few more places: to the lines for your washer, kitchen sink, and your bathroom to start with. If you want, I can see where else you need them and then—"

"That won't be necessary," she said, her tone making her opinion clear of his suggestion. She might be thinking he was trying to take advantage of her. He didn't know and didn't much care.

"Here," and she handed him her credit card, but he held up his hand.

"Sorry, cash only," he answered.

"But I don't have that much on me. Will you take a check?"

Eddie looked at her, noticed the lines of worry on her face, and remembered what Sheila had said. He nodded. "Yeah, sure," and waited as she wrote out the check and handed it over. Shoving it in his back pocket, he picked up his toolbox and then, when it was obvious that she had no intention of saying anything else, just shrugged. "Okay, then. Have a nice day."

Too bad, he thought as he heard the front door slam behind him. He hated leaving a job with a bad taste in his mouth, but some days, that's how it goes. He'd tell Sheila he was done and that would be that. With any luck, that Allison woman wouldn't call him for any more repairs.

"All done," he reported back to Sheila when he reached his next stop. "Not that she seemed all that happy with me, especially when I told her it was cash only. But I let her pay by check. She's good for it, right?"

"Yes, Eddie," the humor in Sheila's tone coming through. "And if it bounces, I'll cover it!"

"Yeah, well, I just hope I don't have to go back there." Although as he said that, he wasn't sure it was true. There was just something about her…

He shook his head. "I did tell her she needed to install some additional valves. I would have even given her a break, but she said no, flat out, like I was trying to rip her off or something. With that kind of suspicious attitude, she's going to find it hard to make friends in this town."

And why do I care? he thought. It isn't my business how she gets on with people!

\#

It was a point that Sheila brought up when she called Amy after talking to Eddie. "I know you've been through a bad time, Amy, and I understand that you are a little short on trust these days. But this isn't like the city you came from. This is a small town where we all know each other. Here in Eden, people do things for each other, help each other out."

When Amy didn't respond, Sheila continued. "And by the way, Eddie changed his schedule for you because I told him it was an emergency. He was supposed to be upgrading the house access for one of our neighbors who can't make the stairs anymore—a job that he was doing at no charge because she's on a fixed income. But he came to your place first. So," she finished with just the smallest hint of reproof in her voice, "it would have been nice if you had shown some appreciation."

"Well, I didn't know that," Amy said defensively, as she took a sip of the coffee that Eddie had brought her. "But you're right. I was rude. Maybe you can tell him I'm sorry."

"Maybe you should tell him yourself," answered Sheila.

"I will, the next time I see him. Although, with any luck, nothing else will break. I can't afford another expense. Not now."

Sheila heard the quaver in her voice that betrayed her stress level. "Well, if something does break, all you have to do is call Eddie and he'll take care of it. Now I've got to go, but if you need anything, let me know. Okay?"

"Okay. And thanks, Sheila—for everything."

#

Amy put down the phone, then pulled out the doughnut from the bag Eddie had brought. Cinnamon-topped, her favorite. Mindful of what Sheila had said, she debated about calling Eddie now to thank him. Or she could just text him. Less embarrassing that way.

But before she could follow through, her phone rang. She knew by the caller ID that it was one of a long line of creditors who were standing in line for money that she didn't have. Sighing, she turned off her phone and went to take her shower. If only it was as easy to wash away her worries.

During the next few weeks, nothing in the house failed that required Eddie's attention, although Amy wasn't certain if she felt relieved or let down. And while Eden was a small village, it was still big enough to prevent her from running into him when she went into town. Regardless of where she shopped—the supermarket, the pharmacy, or the big-box retailer—there was no familiar blue pickup in the parking lot and no glimpse of a jacket covered with motorcycle emblems down any of the aisles.

Just as well, she thought each time she returned home without having seen the elusive handyman, not wanting to ask herself why she was left with a pervasive feeling of disappointment.

That Monday, her destination was the paint store. She wanted to redo her bedroom walls and had decided on a deep blue color called "cerulean skies" that she hoped would create a calming ambiance. These days, she needed all the tranquility she could get. Although Matt had been sentenced to two years in a minimum-security prison for his crime, there were civil suits to contend with, and even after a year, she was still having to deal with attorneys. The result of all this stress was a combination of a bad case of insomnia and a worse case of financial anxiety.

Once home, she carried the paint cans, brushes, painter's tape, and drop cloths into the house and went to work, hoping the physical labor would offset her mental gyrations as she tried to figure out how to pay bills that were more than double the money she had left. And by eight that night, the job was done. Amy stood in the doorway, viewing the results of her labors.

"There, something finally went right," she said aloud, absentmindedly brushing her hair out of her face and leaving behind a streak of blue. "Now all I have to do is clean the brushes and I'm done."

But when she dumped them into the laundry tub and turned on the faucet, the handle kept spinning, letting loose a stream of water that she couldn't stop.

"The shutoff, the shutoff… Where's the shutoff?" she muttered.

But as she traced the pipe from the faucet up the walls and all the way over to the main, there wasn't one to be found. And then she remembered Eddie's suggestion about adding extra valves that she had dismissed without even considering it. Now she was paying the price.

Was it too late to call him? she wondered. But what else could she do?

Quickly, before she could change her mind, she texted him. "Sorry for the late call," she typed. "But I can't get the laundry faucet to stop running, so I had to shut the water off again. Any chance you could come over now and fix it?"

Then, before sending it and mindful of the lecture she had received from Sheila, she added, "Please? I'd really appreciate it" with a smiley-face emoji. Then she sat on the basement step, head in her hands, and waited for his response.

#

"There," Eddie said, stepping back to look at the abstract painting he was doing as his annual Christmas gift to Sheila— a mix of blues: cobalt, Prussian, and lapis lazuli. He'd been so busy working the past few weeks that he kept putting it off. But today was a light day, and once he got home at four, he didn't even stop to eat, but instead went right to his easel.

"A few more strokes," he murmured, but just then he heard the text tone from his phone.

"Now what?" and he resignedly set down his brush and checked the screen. It was from that Allison woman. He hadn't heard from her since he had finished the job a month ago. Under other circumstances, he might have stopped by and checked on how she was doing—the kind of thing that he'd done for other new arrivals to the town—but he wasn't sure how she'd take it.

Still, at odd moments of the day, the thought of her would cross his mind. And even though the last time he saw her she looked like a total wreck, there was still something about her— the way she stood there when he gave her the cost of the tank as though the price was a physical hit, and then after, the way her blue eyes snapped when he suggested more repairs—that made her hard to forget.

I should have given her a break on my labor, he thought as he started to read her message. I've done it before for other people. And by the time he reached the smiley face that closed her text, he had already made up his mind not only to head over right away but to do it for free.

With any luck, it will be a quick fix, he thought as he texted her that he was on his way. And then I can get back home and finally have something to eat, the rumblings of his stomach reminding him that it had been a long time since lunch.

When he arrived, Amy was waiting in the doorway with a tentative smile on her face as though she wasn't sure how he would react. After all, he thought wryly as he went up to the porch, their last meeting hardly ended well. Determined to get things off to a good start, he gave her a grin and said, "Eddie, the plumber, at your service, ma'am" and waited for her response.

Startled, she paused before answering, "Amy, the rude customer, once again in need of your help," and then grinned back, before stepping aside to let him in.

"Well, let's see what we have here," and he followed her down the basement steps. Fortunately, his truck had the items he needed and in less than an hour, the faucet was fixed, and the water was once again flowing through the pipes.

"I was painting," she said, gesturing to the brushes piled in the tub.

"I noticed," and he reached out and touched her forehead where the streak had dried. "Cerulean blue, my favorite color."

She flushed with embarrassment, and then laughed.

"I can tell," she said, wiping away a splotch of blue oil paint from his cheek. "Oh, I'm sorry," her cheeks reddening even more.

Just then, his stomach rumbled, loud enough for both of them to hear. "Sorry. I meant to eat dinner, but I got involved and then, when you called…"

"I took you away from your meal," she finished. "Listen, I haven't eaten either. Would you, I mean, I can fix some eggs and toast if you like."

"Um, sure," surprised by the turn of events.

"And while I'm doing that, would you figure out what other shutoffs I need? I'd like to get them taken care of—when you have time, that is. And then tell me what I owe you for tonight."

"I'll make you a deal. Since you're feeding me, the call will be on the house, okay?" and he watched her face to see how she'd take his suggestion. He was just being friendly, he told himself.

"Okay," and she gave him another quick smile before going up the stairs.

By the time he made his list, the meal was ready. After taking his seat, he pushed his notes over to her.

"It won't be too bad," he explained, as he watched her eyes run down the list. "One shutoff apiece for each water line—hot and cold—going to the bathroom, kitchen, and of course, the laundry room. And I might need some PEX line to replace sections of the old lines, but don't worry. I have some left over from my last job."

While he waited, he took a bite of his eggs. They were done just the way he liked them, he noticed—sunny-side up with the white set, but the yolks still runny.

Then he added. "It should only take an hour," deciding that, even if it ran longer, he'd cover the difference.

"This sounds just fine. Whenever you can get me on your schedule will be great," she said. "Oh, and before I forget, I have an outlet that isn't working, too" and she pointed to the one next to the sink.

He nodded, added it to his list, then pulled out his phone to check his calendar. "How about Friday around four?"

"That would be perfect!" she answered. "Would you like anything else—cookies or something?"

But he shook his head, mopped up the last bit of egg from his dish, and then stood up. "This was plenty, but I better get going. I have an early start. I'll see you the end of the week then. Of course, if something else breaks in the meantime, you can always call me," he added.

She followed him to the door and held out her hand. "Thanks, Eddie," and he took it, held it a moment longer than necessary, then let it go.

"Sleep well," he said and went out to his truck. He'd be back on Friday, he thought, not stopping to ask himself why the week suddenly seemed so long.

#

Amy watched him leave, recalling the dinner they had just shared. How nice it was to sit with someone and enjoy a meal. She couldn't remember the last time she'd done that. If this was what it was like living in a small town—people being friendly and kind and caring—it would work for her.

While she washed the dishes, she thought about the upcoming repair call, telling herself that the glow she felt was because she was dealing with problems like a responsible adult. It was all about getting things fixed. It had nothing to do with who was handling the repairs.

Nevertheless, when Friday arrived, she had decided to bake her favorite dessert: pecan and walnut brownies with powdered sugar topping. While the pan was cooling, she changed out of her sweatpants and t-shirt and into a bright blue jersey and a pair of jeans.

Not that I'm trying to impress him or anything, she told herself as she stroked eyeshadow on her lids and blush across her cheeks. It's just that every time he comes here, I look like a disaster.

She checked the clock and saw it was only three. She still had an hour before he arrived. Should she curl her hair or just pin it up? But before she could decide, she heard the sound of the truck and rushed down the stairs.

"I'm a little early," Eddie said, carrying a box of parts to the porch, "Hope it's okay."

"Yes, sure, no problem," and she smiled. "And when you're done—well, I baked a little something for you. I mean, if you have time. Not that you have to stay to eat it or anything. I mean…" She stopped herself and then laughed. "I'm rattling again. Sorry. I do that when I'm nervous," and then blushed, wishing she could recall the words.

"No need to apologize," he answered as he went into the house. "With any luck, I can knock off these repairs and you'll be in good shape. At least until something else breaks," and he gave her a grin.

And this time, everything went the way it should. The valves were replaced without any issue and the new kitchen outlet performed the way it was supposed to. And if Amy wished that it would have taken a little longer, she ignored the thought.

I'm a customer and he's there to fix whatever needs done, she told herself. The fact that their interaction was on a warmer footing than how it had started was just a bonus.

Amy followed him outside, a plate of brownies in one hand, and watched as he loaded his tools in the truck and wrote up his bill before returning to the porch.

"Here you go," and he handed her the paperwork.

She took it, then held the plate out to him.

"I hope you like them," she said, as he lifted one square to his mouth. Then, as he took a bite, she added, "I made them with pecans and walnuts."

"Oh no," Eddie blurted, and he spit the brownie back out onto the dish.

He rushed to his truck, where he started rummaging through his tool bag, leaving Amy standing there, shocked and confused. She heard him say, "Where is it? Where is it?" and then he yelled to her, "Sorry! I gotta go!"

And before she could say or do anything, he jumped in his truck and roared backward down the drive and out onto the street.

"What the—" and she looked at the plate. There was nothing wrong with them, she knew. She had tasted one herself when she was putting them on the dish! But when she called Sheila to tell her what happened, the mystery was solved.

"Eddie is severely allergic to nuts," Sheila laughed. "He has the full reaction with wheezing and hives and needs a shot from his epinephrine pen right away!"

"Oh, no!" she said. "I might have killed him!"

"Don't blame yourself. There's no way you could have known. But still, it's a good thing he didn't eat too much. You might have had to call 911! Now, while I have you on the phone, I want to invite you to my holiday party. It's Saturday, December 21 at 7 p.m. at my place. Nothing fancy, just drinks and appetizers and desserts. It will give you a chance to meet some of the people in town, too."

"Thanks, Sheila," said Amy. "I'd love to come," not sure why she didn't want to ask if Eddie would be there.

"Great! Now I better call Eddie and make sure he's still alive! Can't afford to lose my go-to handyman!" and with another laugh, Sheila hung up.

Eddie. Should she call him and see if he was okay? And apologize for almost sending him into anaphylactic shock? Or should she just mail his check and hope for the best?

"I'll leave him a message and mail him my payment," she said aloud, dumping the brownies from the dish into the trash.

#

Once back at his place, Eddie grabbed the small tube holding the adrenaline pen from his nightstand and gave himself a shot. Almost immediately, he could feel the allergy symptoms subside. Unfortunately, his embarrassment over what happened remained. Had he also spit the brownie bits on her? And what did she think when he took off without an explanation? Was she mad at him? Should he call and say he was sorry?

Before he could make up his mind, his phone rang. It was Amy, but not sure what to say, Eddie took the coward's way out and let it go to voice mail.

I'll listen to it later, he decided, and then, almost immediately, there came a text from Sheila: "Still alive?" with a winking emoji.

"Yeah, yeah," he said, calling her back. "I had left my allergy pen at home and had to go get it. So, I guess she told you," waiting to hear what else Amy might have said.

"Yes, and she felt absolutely terrible about it. But I told her it wasn't her fault. By the way, I also invited her to my Christmas party—just in case you were wondering."

"Oh," he said.

"So, you have almost a month to figure out how you're going to react when you see her. You know, it's not like you, Eddie. You're not usually so, so—well, however it is you're being," she observed.

"Yeah, well, I don't usually spit on my customers either," he said, and then flushed again as he thought about it.

Sheila laughed. "Well, there's a first time for everything!"

Yes, there was, Eddie thought later, as he listened to the message Amy had left. She apologized, said she was mailing his check, apologized again, and then ended her message without saying anything else.

He had never had such a strong reaction to a woman before. Oh, there were ones that he dated, and even a few relationships that he thought might go further. But then, for whatever reason, he still ended up on his own. What was it about Amy that was different? And why did it matter?

He sent her a quick text saying he was fine, no worries, and then fixed himself a plate of toast and eggs. But that didn't help put her out of his thoughts, since it brought to mind the meal they had shared.

Damn it! Eddie dropped his dinner in the trash and went to his easel. He might as well finish Sheila's painting. He'd just drop it off when it was done and skip the party.

#

Amy spent the rest of November and early December alternately working on her finances and painting the rest of the rooms in her house. She had to do something to keep herself busy, even though she couldn't stop thinking about Eddie.

Would he be at Sheila's party? And if he was, what should she say? His last text was pretty abrupt—just a few lines. He probably saw her as one problem after another: first her terrible attitude when they met and then damn near killing him with her dessert.

Not that it had been all bad, she reminded herself. That dinner they had was nice—no pressure, just two people eating eggs and toast. But no chance of that happening again. He'd never trust another meal at her place!

The day before Sheila's party, Amy went back into the city to get her hair cut and find something nice to wear to the event. After all, she thought as she spent way more than she had planned on a black silk top and matching skirt, this is the first time I'll be meeting some of these people. I just want to make a good impression, trying to ignore the little voice that said there was only one person whose opinion she really cared about.

The next evening, carrying a bottle of expensive wine as a hostess gift, Amy arrived at the party. As she got out of her car, she scanned the driveway, but when she didn't see Eddie's pickup among the other vehicles, did her best to quell her disappointment.

"Merry Christmas!" The greeting came from Sheila, standing in the doorway. "Thanks, but you needn't have," taking the bottle with one hand as she led Amy into the house with the other. "Now come in and meet everyone!"

Holiday lights draped the windows and carols were playing softly in the background. Amy followed Sheila as she introduced her to the others, but she was only paying half attention to the names and faces. There was only one person she wanted to see, and he wasn't there.

As she went over to the table for a glass of punch, she heard Sheila call out behind her.

"You're late! But I forgive you."

Amy turned and there he was, holding a large flat package wrapped in holiday paper.

"I hope you like it. I remember you said you were a fan of abstract art so that's what I did," Eddie said and handed it to Sheila.

As she unwrapped it, Amy could see the blue swirls across the canvas, both calming and yet exciting, peaceful yet full of movement.

"It's beautiful," she blurted.

Eddie looked up and saw her and then blushed. "Well, I'm not a professional or anything. I just like to paint what I feel," he said awkwardly.

"But it really is lovely," she answered, and then Sheila pushed him forward.

"Get yourself something to drink," she commanded. "I'm going to put this painting somewhere where everyone can see it," and with that she left them standing together.

"Punch?" Amy asked, and when he nodded, she filled his glass. Then the two of them walked through the French door leading to the back deck.

"Have you been here long?" asked Eddie.

Amy shook her head. "No, I just arrived. I didn't know you painted," and then regretted saying that, as though she had a right to know something about his private life. But he didn't seem to mind.

"It's something I do just for me and sometimes for other people. Can't make a living at it, but then, that's what my job is for, I guess."

"Well, I think you're a terrific artist," she said. "And I love the colors you chose. Is that what you were working on when you came over that evening—you know, when I was painting?" She wanted to say, "when we had a meal together," but decided against it.

"Yeah, I wanted to make sure to get it done so the oil would be dry." He looked over at her. "Listen, about what happened—"

But she stopped him. "I'm just glad you survived my dessert!" and she gave him her best smile.

He smiled back. "So, are you ready for the holidays?" changing the subject.

"Not really. I mean, it's not like I'll be spending it with anyone."

Deciding that sounded too pathetic, she added, "It's not like when I was a child. My family would drive up to Maine to visit my grandparents and they always had a big Douglas fir on the porch all lit up. You could see it from blocks away! That always meant Christmas to me."

"No tree this year?" he asked hesitantly.

She shook her head. "No, and not much Christmas spirit either, I'm afraid. It's just—" and then impulsively she told him what her ex-husband had done and why she left the city where they had lived.

"It was so humiliating," she said, looking out over the snowy backyard. "People either felt sorry for me or, if they were someone he had stolen from, blamed me for what he did. I just couldn't take it, so after the divorce, I sold the condo at a loss and came here where no one knew."

But before Eddie could say anything, the door opened behind them.

"There you two are!" said Sheila. "Come on in and get some food while it's hot!"

As Amy stepped forward, her heel slipped on the snow and Eddie reached out to steady her.

"Let me help you," and he took her hand in his. But once inside, Eddie was stopped by one of the guests who needed his opinion on roofing material, while Amy was pulled into a debate over cutout cookies versus nut rolls. By the time she made it down the line at the food table, she had lost sight of Eddie.

"He got a call and had to leave," Sheila said as she handed her a glass of eggnog.

Had she noticed I was looking for him? Amy wondered. "I just wanted to wish him a happy holiday," she said. "He's been very, well, kind to me" and got a knowing look in return.

"Uh, huh. Well, you can always call him, you know, to tell him that. It doesn't always have to be about work."

Amy just nodded and then set down her empty plate and glass. "I really had a great time, Sheila. Thanks for inviting me. But I think I'm going to leave. It looks like it's starting to snow, and I'd rather go while the roads are clear."

She gave Sheila a hug and then retrieved her coat and hat. It had been a very nice party and all the people were so warm and friendly. So why did she suddenly feel so deflated? If Eddie hadn't had to leave… but she stopped herself. An emotional involvement was the last thing she needed right now, she decided. She was just letting the holiday memories get to her.

#

Eddie looked for Amy to explain his early departure, but he couldn't find her in the crowd. So, he grabbed his jacket and drove over to Mrs. Carlson's house to get her furnace running again. It was the third time he had to fix it, but he knew she didn't have the money to replace it. But while he was cleaning the pilot light and ignition sensor, lubricating the blower motor and shaft bearings, and adjusting the burners, he was remembering what Amy had told him—not just about her divorce but about Christmas at her grandparents.

By the time he was done, and heat was once again traveling through the ductwork, he had made up his mind to buy Amy a small pine tree, decorate it with some lights, and leave it as a surprise on her front porch Christmas Eve. Then all she'd have to do is bring it into the house and plug it in.

It won't fix everything that's wrong in her life, he thought, but at least she'd have something to brighten her Christmas morning.

And Eddie's plan would have worked except that he almost slipped carrying the tree up the porch steps. The snow had started that morning, and while kids looked forward to a white Christmas, the combination of snow and darkness made stairs treacherous, resulting in him setting the tree down with a heavy thump.

The porch lights came on, and before he had a chance to make his retreat, Amy had opened the door.

"I thought… well, I don't know what I thought but what are you doing here? Oh!" catching sight of the tree.

"Merry Christmas," Eddie said awkwardly, brushing the snow from his knees. "Should I bring it in?"

"Yes, please!" with an expression on her face like a young girl who had just seen Santa.

Carefully, Eddie carried it across the threshold, then stood there, waiting. "Where do you want it?" he asked finally.

"How about in the living room? We could put it on here," and she moved some books from the table in front of the window. "I think there's an outlet somewhere. Oh, here it is!"

"Perfect," and Eddie carefully set it down before straightening the tiny blue star at the very top. "Now all I have to do is plug it in, flip the switch, and it will be all ready to enjoy."

But the result wasn't what was expected. As soon as he turned on the tree lights, everything went dark: the two lamps on either side of the couch, the ceiling light in the entryway, and even the hall fixture.

"Well, that's not good," Eddie said under his breath and glanced over at Amy. He could barely make out her expression in the moonlight that streamed through the window. Was she angry? "You know, with any luck, it's just another bad outlet" and waited for her to say something.

She was silent for another minute or two, and then moved closer to him. "As it happens," she said, lightly touching his arm, "I know this great handyman. He can fix anything. And he's a really sweet guy, too. With any luck, he's available right now."

"It just so happens he is." And without another word, Eddie went out to his truck for what he needed. In short order, the outlet was replaced, the breaker reset, and they were back in the now brightly lit living room.

"Ready to try again?" he asked her.

"Wait. Let me shut off the other lights first. That way we'll get the full effect."

Once she returned, Eddie plugged in the cord and then, mentally crossing his fingers, flipped the switch, turning the small tree into a pyramid of glittering white lights.

"I guess your luck held," he said, glancing down at her.

"I guess it did," she agreed. "Thank you for a lovely Christmas present," reaching up to kiss him on the cheek.

But just then he turned to face her, and their lips met.

"My pleasure," he said when they broke apart. "Merry Christmas, Amy."

"Merry Christmas, Eddie," she answered, and as he put his arm around her, she leaned her head against his shoulder, watching their reflection in the window as the snow gently fell.

BINGO

"Come on! You'll like it! It's fun!"

In the five years we had been together, I had heard those words from Tally's mouth more times than I cared to count, and each time, I had learned the hard way that her version of fun wasn't at all like mine. Like when she convinced me that bungee-jumping from the top of a renovated roller-coaster would be fun and so I agreed—only to find out that vomiting while hanging upside down is not on my top ten list of activities I want to repeat.

Then there was the couples cooking classes—"Learn how to make famous Italian specialties while enjoying vino from the different regions"—that she promised would be an unforgettable experience. And I have to admit she was right. It is hard to forget the result of an incredibly sharp de-boning knife coming in contact with the tender skin of your palm that ended up as a two-inch long wound, which, according to the ER doctor as he merrily stitched away "just missed taking off your pinkie! You'll have a cool scar though!"

The last one—an eight-hour bike ride followed by a relaxing night in a Victorian inn—should have been as romantic as the brochure had promised. But what Tally hadn't taken into account (and how could she, given the difference in our physiology?) was the consequence of having a majority of my weight divvied up between my shoulders and my butt for that length of time.

By the time we reached our room, I could barely move my head, thanks to a pinched nerve in my neck, while my "manhood" was feeling the effects of reduced blood flow and refused to rise to the occasion, so to speak.

So I gave her "It's fun!" statement about as much credence as I would if it was uttered by an IRS agent proposing to review my last ten years' worth of returns, and just considered what I knew about the activity itself.

Bingo: a simple game played by mostly senior citizens that didn't involve anything more energetic than marking paper squares with colored daubers—an activity that couldn't possibly be life-threatening, unless winning a round brought on a heart attack.

The worst I could get was a paper cut, I reasoned, and besides, Tally looked so cute standing there all excited, wearing her special "I am a Bingo Baby!" sweatshirt and holding her little red and white checked bingo bag filled with markers and God knows what else. And she had even made my favorite supper: lasagna with meat sauce and lots of hot peppers. How could I refuse such a simple request?

Besides, it was the only thing Tally did for fun that didn't include me, and was, in fact, something she had been playing since she was old enough to know her letters and numbers, thanks to her Gramma Billie who was a bingo fanatic. (How much of a bingo fanatic was brought home to me when they buried her with her special dauber—a fluorescent purple one—and held her wake not at a restaurant but at her favorite bingo hall.)

Considering that Tally not only sat through every NFL game every year and kept me well supplied with nachos and beer while I watched the tackles, touchdowns, and two-point conversions on my far from adequate (in my opinion) 30-inch-screen television, I figured I owed it to her.

The bottom line was that I loved Tally and wanted to make her happy. And because of that, and keeping in mind that she had cut up all those hot peppers with her tender little fingers, I was willing to give it a shot—especially when, right before we left, she showed me the new nightgown she had bought at Lovely Ladies' Lingerie: black and lacy with ribbon ties.

What thirty-year-old male can resist the promise of sexual favors in return for just playing a simple game for an hour or two?

So an hour later, I found myself sandwiched between a large old lady, whose bizarre collection of tchotchkes (a paper umbrella with a slightly pineapple-rum smell to it, a misshapen piece of white pottery, and a pocket Bible) kept drifting over into the 16-inch section allotted to me, and some young guy who had enough body piercings and tattoos to qualify him for the local motorcycle gang.

Not that I had much of a choice of where to sit. As soon as we entered the church hall (a good forty-five minutes before the night's activities were due to start), Tally had made a beeline for what she referred to as "her" table—despite the fact that there were plenty of spaces open at the sixty odd tables that filled the room. She took what was clearly her usual seat, across from me and next to an old guy who greeted her with a big hug and kiss on the cheek.

"Hi, Charlie," she said, kissing him right back, and then waved a hand in my direction. "This is Bobby—"

"Her boyfriend," I said, emphasizing the last word, just in case she wasn't going to continue.

Not that I was worried about somebody who was old enough to be my grandfather, although I wasn't all that crazy about the subsequent attention Charlie gave her. He helped her off with her jacket, complimented her on her hair (which was only pulled back in a scrunchy) and told her how great she smelled—a load of crap since Tally never used cologne. I knew that because the big bottles I bought her every Christmas, birthday, and Valentine's Day from the corner drugstore were still sitting unopened on her dresser.

The two of them chatted while Tally opened her bag and set out her lucky pieces: a little plastic elf, a ceramic mouse missing part of its tail, and a wind-up rabbit. Then, she lined up her bingo sheets—three cards for each of the ten border colors—and with great precision, taped their edges together. (I, on the other hand, had just one each, which made me feel more than a little inadequate.) Then came her daubers: yellow, green, pink, orange, red, and of course, lavender—"For Gramma Billie," she explained.

I would have set out mine except that I didn't have any—something the old guy noticed right away.

"Where's your markers?" he asked. "You can't play without them, you know!" as though I was stupid enough to try.

At that, Tally looked up, frowned quickly, and then looked back at her own collection. She picked up her orange one first, set it down, and then, after what was clearly much mental debate, reluctantly pushed the yellow dauber across the table to me, with the instructions to "mark your free spots."

And I did—or tried to, anyway. But I must have pressed the tip down too firmly on the first card's center square, because somehow the damned dauber slipped from my fingers and skidded across two adjacent squares, leaving behind a yellow smear that rendered that card useless and forced me to spend another 10 bucks for a whole new set. (Apparently you can't buy just one card but have to purchase them in sets of ten—a point that was made quite clear to me when I handed over a crumpled one-dollar bill, and the bingo monitor, with the attitude of a bookie, stood there with his palm outstretched and waited for the rest of my cash.)

After making it back to my seat and being much more careful where I put my dauber and with what force (which, in retrospect sounds like what an adolescent male would read in a sex-for-dummies manual), I was ready for the first game.

"The ball will show in the monitor," Tally said, pointing to the screen, "but remember, if that's the number you need to win, don't yell 'Bingo' until he actually calls it, or it won't count" which seemed rather nitpicky to me. I mean, if it was the winning number, why not say so right away?

But I nodded as though it all made perfect sense.

The caller took his seat, turned on the machine, and shouted, "Let's play bingo! Our first game of the night is single bingo!"

"That's five across, five down, or five diagonally," Tally whispered, as though I was too stupid to figure it out for myself, I thought with a flash of irritation. I daubed B-3, O-72, and N-38, and then, after a few balls were called that didn't match any of my squares, I-22 and G-53. At least, that was what I *thought* he had said, and so I yelled "Bingo!" once he announced the ball.

As it turned out, it was G-52—an error that the caller made public to the entire room by stating "That is not a good bingo," with a little more emphasis than I thought was necessary, once one of his cohorts verified my mistake.

"Geez, buddy," muttered the delinquent on my left while the elderly player on my other side contented herself with a sniff of superiority at my stupidity.

"That's okay, Bobby," Tally said, and squeezed my hand with her left one, giving me what comfort she could while simultaneously daubing her final square with her right, which resulted in a horizontal row of orange blobs and a $20 cash award.

I congratulated Tally on her win, crumpled up my card, and resolved to do better. After all, if this was all it took to win, surely I could redeem myself! And it would give Tally and me some new, non-horizontal activity to share.

I was doing it for her, I said to myself, although the prospect of winning the choice of the evening's grand prize—a 70-inch television or a year's worth of free bingo games for two—was certainly an extra incentive.

"Now we move on to the double bingo," the caller announced, and I stopped daydreaming about which wall would be the best one for that brand-new big screen and hurriedly set out another sheet—and then quickly changed it for the correct one after Mr. Tattoo hissed, "The blue border one, not red, stupid."

I caught Tally's eye and she smiled at me—the same smile, I realized, that she gave to the pizza delivery guy when he couldn't figure out in his head how much change he owed her. I grimaced back, resolving to show her that I wasn't the complete bingo idiot I appeared to be.

I'd win this game, I vowed. And what's more, I'd win that damned grand prize too! And I'd even let her download her favorite forties tear-jerkers onto it, as long as it didn't interfere with any of the games I watched.

But while I didn't call "Bingo" when I shouldn't have, I missed the chance to say it when I did have it, which was pointed out to me three balls later by the old lady—after she had won, of course.

"You know, you had a double bingo two balls ago," pointing to the four marked squares—one in each corner—and then the diagonal line of colored daubs running from the top of the "B" column to the last one under "O." "Four corners counts."

"Oh, sweetie, didn't I explain that to you?" said Tally, as she whipped out her next set of cards. "I'm sorry. I guess I thought you knew!"

And how would I? I thought to myself a little testily. I'd never played this stupid game before!

"Here," said the old guy, pushing a paper across the table. "This might help. It lists the types of games and what counts for each."

I muttered a quick thanks and tried to give myself a crash course in Bingo 101, doing my best to figure out what "picture frame," "Super T," and "crazy kite" were, which put me two balls behind in the latest game: a postage stamp one. But ultimately, and after whipping my head around repeatedly from the table to the monitor to the display board, I was pretty confident that I had daubed every legitimate square, even if it did make that nerve in my neck start to hurt again and I still wasn't sure what "postage stamp" meant, let alone if I had one.

Someone else did though—and I couldn't decide if I was disappointed or relieved when I heard "Bingo!" hollered by a very pregnant lady two tables over. There was a brief delay while she collected her winnings and, assisted by two seatmates, moaned and groaned her way to the exit, pausing every three minutes to do the "Hoo-hoo-hoo" breathing pattern that anybody who has been part of the birth process (or watched some version of it on television) would recognize as the "Better get to the hospital because that kid is on his way!" stage.

Once that excitement was over, the games resumed: a round of single bingo followed by a double and an X game. Then people started getting up, which I foolishly thought signaled the end of the evening and the beginning—at least from my way of looking at it, remembering the nightie—of something far more enjoyable.

But just as I began dumping my unused sheets into a nearby wastebasket, Tally stopped me. "It's just break time, Bobby. You know, for bathroom and smoke runs. We still have the rest of the night to go."

Shit. That meant there was at least ninety more minutes of B-1s and O-70s, not to mention all the numbers in the I, N and G columns, to sit through. But I manned up, restacked my cards, and reminded myself of how hard Tally must have worked on dinner. Although in the back of my mind, I wondered why her manicured nails didn't show signs of hard labor, where that large foil baking pan had come from, and whether it was just my imagination that the lasagna tasted an awful lot like Mama Rosa's from down the street.

Ninety minutes. I could do that, I told myself—for Tally and our relationship and that black nightgown.

Well, the road to hell and all that—the second half of the evening involved games that challenged my geometric comprehension. There was the Crazy T set, followed by the Large Picture Frame (and of course, right after, the Small Picture Frame), the Flag round, and then the Y, U and F games. There wasn't a pattern they didn't use and a game I didn't lose, although Tally and Charlie had more than their fair share of bingos between them, and even the two on either side of me racked up a win each.

Finally, and not soon enough as far as I was concerned, came the last game of the night: a combination coverall and lightning round. This was for the biggee, the 70-inch television—*my* 70-inch television, I kept telling myself, picturing it in our living room displaying every tackle and end zone touchdown made by my favorite team.

"Get ready, Bobby!" Tally whispered and then, after a warning from the caller that there was to be "no talking and there'll be no letters called—only numbers," the game began.

I did my best to keep up, but unfortunately, it didn't take long before I was several balls behind, owing to the fact that I had no idea which number was in which row. What made it worse was that the old lady next to me, who was playing twelve cards to my single, was breezing along, smacking her dauber down with undisguised glee on the last one while I was still doing the bingo version of hunt-and-peck on my first card.

And then it happened. I had one spot still undaubed. And so, I noticed, did Tally. In my case, it was B-4 while hers was O-70.

Three more balls, while we both waited, daubers at the ready. And then, there it was—a big, beautiful B-4 showing up on the monitor. I marked my spot and got ready to shout "Bingo!" all the while thinking how jealous my buddies would be when they came over to watch football on that big, beautiful 70-inch screen.

I watched the monitor, where the ball—my ball, as I had come to think of it—was removed and replaced by the next one. I waited for the caller to announce "B-4," calculated the size of the television versus the capacity of my Datsun's trunk, and then saw the identifying marks on the new one: O-70.

It was Tally's ball, the one she was waiting for.

But even if I hadn't known it was the one that she needed, her sharp intake of breath and the little beads of sweat on her forehead would have given it away. I opened my mouth, shut it again, and when the kid next to me started saying "Hey, stupid, you're a—" I jabbed him so hard with my elbow that he fell off his folding chair.

Tally glanced at me and then at my sheet, and I just shrugged and smiled at her, indicating in my manly way that my love for her trumped my desire to win. Then the caller said, "O-70!" and, after blowing me a little kiss, Tally yelled "Bingo!" making her the single prize winner of the evening, while I sat there, thinking how much I loved her—and football—and hoping that she loved me at least enough to choose the right prize.

And she did—the right prize from her perspective, at least—which is why I'll be spending the next twelve months in that crowded church hall daubing paper squares with my very own light blue marker.

But it's not all bad news, since I know that underneath her standard "I am a Bingo Baby!" sweatshirt and jeans, Tally will be wearing an even more special (from my perspective, at least) article of clothing: a red satin teddy, reserved just for the occasion.

Bingo.

FOR THE FIRST TIME–AGAIN

"Hello."

Jack turned, startled by a voice he hadn't heard for—how long? Four years? Five?

She was standing there, smiling uncertainly, as though unsure of his response. After all, he remembered, the last time they had spoken, acrimonious words were exchanged and tears were shed.

Her tears—*he* was incapable of showing emotion, Rachel had said. "You're like a damned machine, Jack! Why can't you say how you feel? Don't you love me?"

He had stood there, silent, until she had walked away. It wasn't until it was too late that he knew the answer.

"Hello," Rachel repeated, her smile fading. "How have you been?"

"Fine, just fine," the words coming automatically. "You look good. You look very good," and then, idiotically, Jack held out his hand when what he really wanted to do was take her in his arms.

"I hate these trade shows, but it was my turn to go to one," she said, ignoring his outstretched hand. She looked past his shoulder as though searching for someone. That's how they had met—at a trade show, two strangers from the same town meeting a thousand miles from home. "But at least the food is good."

Jack clutched at the opening she had so carelessly tossed out. "There's a special dinner planned for tonight—Korean, I think. Are you going?"

"I suppose."

He watched Rachel's fingers tracing the delicate silver links of her bracelet. He had bought it for her after they had been together for a year—slipped it around her slender wrist and kissed her. Two months later, they were shouting at each other in an empty parking lot, while a wet November snow rained icy tears on her dark curling hair. "Would you like to go with me?"

She pushed the bracelet under the sleeve of her long sweater. Then she faced him squarely, without a smile.

"I'll see you there," and she turned and was gone.

The rest of the day passed in a blur. Jack met with sales representatives, heard them praise their latest designs and newest products but later couldn't remember a single word. His suit coat pocket bulged with business cards and brochures, his face ached from the effort of maintaining a smile.

Even a hot shower couldn't wash away the depression that had overtaken him. All Jack could remember was the way she had looked at him, coolly and without emotion. She was just being kind, he thought to himself as he closed the door to the motel room behind him. She probably didn't care if she ever saw him again.

#

"Damn it, why didn't I pack the red dress?"

Rachel stood there in front of her suitcase, hair still damp from the shower, her robe belted tightly around her. She *should* have packed the red dress. She should have gone to the hairdresser—had her hair permed, even colored. The gray hairs were coming in faster than she had expected.

"Why do I care?" she said aloud, but then turned to regard her reflection critically. The truth was she *did* care. It may have been five years since they had seen each other but she wanted to look the same. No, she wanted to look better. She wanted *him* to want her again. But what did *she* want?

The alarm on her phone buzzed warningly. She had less than an hour before dinner—barely enough time to do her nails and hair, come up with a great outfit, shave half a decade off her looks.

"Oh, the hell with it," and she pulled out her running suit from the bottom of the stack. She would go for a walk on the beach, clear her head, get herself in better order. The past was past and she had made the right decision. He had been too cold, too emotionless, leaving passion up to her. She was the one who offered hugs and kisses, the one who was the last to let go after they made love.

"But not this time," Rachel promised herself as she waited for the elevator. "I'll be the cool one. And after all, it's not like we're going to be seeing each other again. This is just a fluke— a chance meeting. Nothing is going to happen between us."

The walk did her good, but Rachel had cut her time too closely. She barely had enough time to take a quick shower and curl her hair. Nevertheless, in her black dress and heels, she looked, well, if not glamorous, at least presentable. Besides, she reminded herself, it didn't matter. The room would be crowded. They probably wouldn't even see each other.

Twisting to view her back in the mirror, she caught sight of the hem. It was uneven, and when she took off her dress, she saw the thread had let go.

"Damn it!" and Rachel stamped her foot in frustration. That was the only dress she brought, and she had neglected to pack her little sewing kit. "Well, that's it, then. I won't go. I'll go back to the beach and watch the moon rise. I'm sure he'll find someone else to sit with."

Coward, her image mocked her, but she turned her back to the mirror and throwing the dress on the bed, she reached again for the sweatpants and shirt she had discarded.

It was better this way, Rachel thought. Safer. It had taken her a long time to get over losing him. She didn't need that much pain, that much emotion again. The first time had been hard enough. Better for her to keep her distance.

#

As the evening wore on, Jack toyed mechanically with his food, his eyes rarely leaving the door, hoping against hope that she would arrive.

"Isn't this food wonderful?" It was the blonde sitting next to him. She had taken the empty seat sometime between the third course and the fourth, and apparently felt compelled to comment on each menu item. He didn't even have to respond. He just had to be there.

"I just love these ethnic meals, don't you?" she chattered on, dropping bits of mushroom on the tablecloth. She insisted on using the chopsticks they had provided, and, as a consequence, more food ended up on the floor and table than in her mouth.

"Sure, they're fine," he said. A movement past the glass door caught his eye. Was that—? "If you'll excuse me, I need to make a phone call. The office," he added vaguely, and tossing down his napkin, Jack left the table.

#

"I should have gone in."

There was no one around to hear her berate herself. It was ridiculous. She could have been eating a warm meal instead of walking on a cold beach, getting a sinus headache from the damp air. Or if she had taken a different route to the lobby instead of the one that led past the dining room, she wouldn't have seen him apparently enjoying the company of that blonde.

"So, what if he is?" she said aloud. "I don't care what he does or who he's with! I'm over him! It was just that I was surprised to see him. That's all."

Her cheeks were wet—sea spray, she told herself. That's all it was.

"I might as well go back in," and Rachel turned to retrace her steps to the motel. Then she saw him, waiting.

"You missed dinner." His voice gave her no clue as to his feelings.

"I know," she answered, and then, the words, unbidden, "*You* seemed to be having a good time."

"I waited for you," he went on, ignoring her words. "I thought… I hoped you were having second thoughts."

"About dinner?" Rachel asked mockingly.

"About us," and Jack drew closer. "You said once that I lacked emotion. I didn't. I just lacked the ability to show it until it was too late. And there hasn't been a day since then that I haven't thought of you, a night that I haven't regretted what happened."

She stood there, shivering in the night air, almost afraid of what she was hearing. She didn't want to be hurt again. It had been a long time ago. It would be safer to keep it as a memory.

"When I saw you," and he swallowed hard, "it was like the first time. I want it to be the first time again."

She turned away, looking at the beach. The tide had turned, and even now was running up on the shore, washing away the footprints she had made and leaving the sand smooth and unmarked.

Jack moved to her side and put his arm around her. "I missed you," and his arm tightened. "I don't want to miss you anymore."

Rachel turned to look at him, letting his arm fall from her shoulder. "I can't go through this again," she said, her voice low and unsteady. "I don't want to relive the past or begin where we left off."

"I understand" and he held out his hand. "But this time it's different. *I'm* different. We aren't picking up the pieces— we're starting fresh. It will be for the first time."

"For the first time," she echoed and then took his hand. "For the first time—again."

COUPLES

DOORS AND WINDOWS

"Get away from the window. And close those curtains!" Melanie's words came out harsher than she had intended, and hurriedly she tried to soften her tone. "It's cold outside and this house is so drafty. At least the drapes block some of that wind. And I don't want you to get sick," she added belatedly.

She felt rather than heard Carolee's almost inaudible sigh, felt rather than heard her daughter's rejection of not just the words but of the message behind them: He's not just late. He's not coming—just like last week, and the week before that and the week before that.

"Carolee?" she tried again, but when the nine-year-old didn't respond, didn't even turn around, she moved away from the doorway and headed down the stairs to the kitchen. She'd make her daughter's favorite Sunday afternoon snack: hot cocoa and cinnamon toast. And then they could play a board game or watch a movie or…

Or just sit and stare at each other, with Carolee blaming her mother for her father's absence, and Melanie wondering if her daughter would ever understand, would ever forgive her, or, for that matter, if she had done the right thing in the first place.

#

Carolee heard her mother's footsteps and for a moment, thought to follow her. But her bedroom window was the only place where she had a good view of the road. From there she could watch for her father's pickup truck and have enough time to slip on her winter coat and hat and be ready to run out the door as he pulled in the driveway. Everything was laid out on the bed: her jacket, stocking cap, gloves and scarf, her backpack with her homework. Sometimes when they were sitting at Bill's Burger Barn, her father would help her with her math.

That's why she hadn't even opened her textbook. All her other assignments were completed, but she had saved math for last. In case they had time to do it. In case he came.

"And he will come," she murmured, moving away from the window so she could rub her forehead. It was cold where she had leaned it against the glass.

But she was only half-convinced. The court order defining the terms of the separation—the one she had found months ago when she was looking for a paper clip on her mother's desk—had been clear: a visit each Sunday from noon to five and one weekend a month from Saturday at nine in the morning until Sunday night at eight. Each week she marked off the dates that she saw her father, and if some months had fewer crossed-off blocks than others, she blamed it on the weather or her father's work schedule or, if her parents had fought the weekend before, her mother.

But it was already half-past three and she had been waiting since twelve. Her stomach was rumbling. She was getting hungry, but she wouldn't go downstairs and eat, even though she could now smell the aroma of the hot chocolate wafting up the stairs. Her mother made it the old-fashioned way with cocoa and milk and sugar, and since last Friday was payday, there might even be a tiny mountain of whipped cream swirled on top. And cinnamon toast, as many slices as she wanted.

Carolee's mouth watered, but she fought the urge to abandon her post. If she did, if she went downstairs and drank her cocoa and ate her toast, she would be admitting to a truth that she didn't want to face: her father wasn't coming. So, she held firm and kept watching the road, now coated with a thin sheen of ice.

#

It was the ice that was to blame, Rob said to himself. The ice and the truck's more-than-slightly bald tires and the fact that he had to jump the battery just to get the vehicle started. Ever since the plant closed down and he lost his job, ever since the landlord finally kicked him out—not that he could blame him, since he was three months late with his rent—ever since he had moved into the shelter, he knew it was only a matter of time before the pickup would fail him.

Then he'd have to take a bus for the hour-long trip back to the town where he used to live, back to where the three of them once were a family. And when he got there, find some explanation for why he couldn't take his daughter out for a three-dollar kid's meal at the hamburger place, or why Carolee couldn't come stay the weekend with him or why—this to Melanie—the check was late. Again.

The ice—that was the problem. As for the rest, he would have to tell Melanie the truth. He had run out of excuses, run out of reasons, run out of justifications for everything, even if not all of it was his fault.

But the closer he came to the highway exit, the more afraid he grew of what would happen next. What Melanie would say. What Carolee would think.

And so he had finally surrendered to the fear and pulled off onto the side of the road and sat there, shaking, wondering how everything had gone so wrong when all he had wanted was a job and a house and a wife and child. And love.

#

It was quarter to four when Carolee heard, rather than saw, her father's pickup: the sound of the exhaust escaping through the holes in the muffler, the grinding of the gears as he downshifted. She knew the sound of the truck as well as she knew her own heartbeat, and without waiting to see the vehicle, to hear the cab door creak open and then shut, Carolee pulled on her coat and hat, grabbed her belongings and headed downstairs.

But then she stopped on the last step, the anger emanating from the kitchen, from her mother, an almost palpable force.

"You're late! Again! Damn it, Rob! She's been waiting for hours, and she wouldn't even eat! Couldn't you have called?"

Carolee heard a low rumble of words and knew it was her father trying to calm down her mother. It wouldn't work. It never did. It didn't work when they all lived together, and it wouldn't work now. Best she go in so they would stop, and the visit—what was left of it anyway—could start.

"You're right, Melanie, but wait. I need to explain. I need to tell you something—" Rob stopped when he saw his daughter in the doorway. He didn't want to finish the conversation in front of her, didn't want her to hear that her father was jobless, homeless, a failure as a man, a husband, and a parent.

He pasted a smile on his face and opened his arms wide, and when she ran into them, he hugged her close and just kept saying, "How's my girl? How's my sweetheart? I've missed you so much!"

Melanie stood there and then for a moment, she was suddenly back in her hospital room, watching her husband hold their newborn daughter—the child they had created out of love and hope—with a look on his face that was a mix of awe and fierce protectiveness. The same look he had now, except there was a slash of pain underscoring it, the same pain she felt each time he left and she saw her daughter's anguish at his departure.

She turned away, swallowing hard, and put on a pot of coffee. While they were gone for what little time remained, she'd go through the stack of bills, measuring the total due against her pitifully small paycheck, and wonder what she would do if the rumors were true and Wayside Market would shut down the first of the year. Unemployment wouldn't be all that much, and her weekend work at Sam's Bar & Grille would hardly make up the difference. As for the child support…

And with that, her anger returned, and she pushed the start button on the coffeemaker with more force than necessary.

"I'm ready to go, Daddy."

Melanie turned at her daughter's words just in time to see Rob shake his head.

"Not today, sweetie," he said and led her to the table where her now cold cocoa and toast were waiting. "The roads are really slippery and the wind is sharp," knowing even as he spoke that the excuses he offered weren't enough. But they'd have to be. All he had in his wallet was a ten-dollar bill and he needed that for gas.

"Tell you what," slipping her coat off her shoulders. "Let's sit here and work together on whatever homework you have to finish. Okay?"

Carolee nodded although it wasn't okay. It wasn't what she wanted: the three of them in the kitchen. The room was too small to hold all the emotions: her mother's anger, her father's fear that she sensed even if she didn't understand its cause, and her own disappointment.

But at least he was here, she told herself as she pulled out her math book and paper and pencil. He was here and that was all that mattered.

And while the two of them struggled through the calculations—Rob patiently explaining how to understand the problem and arrive at a solution—Melanie made a fresh mug of cocoa and more toast for her daughter. And then, almost as an afterthought, poured a cup of coffee for Rob—black with two sugars—and set it next to his elbow.

His shirt was missing a button and his hair was longer than he usually wore it, she noticed, and there was a slight whiff of sweat from him when he moved his arm to pull Carolee's book closer. And his face… There was something about it: the way his cheekbones caught the light, the shadow on his chin where he had missed shaving.

Unkempt. That was the word she was searching for. You would think he would at least make himself presentable, especially since he hadn't seen his daughter for nearly a month.

She sat down across from them, trying with limited success to calm her anger.

"I'll never get it!" Carolee said in frustration, as once again her father looked at her answer, shook his head, and then slid the paper back to her side of the table. "I hate math!"

"That's okay, sweetie," Rob said, trying to console her. "Think how good you are at art! You draw wonderful pictures. Besides, no one is good at everything. I'm a terrible speller and your mom isn't any good at math either."

He quickly glanced up at Melanie with a smile, hoping she wouldn't take offense and, caught off guard, she smiled back.

It was true, Melanie thought. Each month, Rob would be the one to balance their checkbook because, try as she might, the figures never came out the way they should. But he never blamed her, just sat there with his hot chocolate and cinnamon toast—and was that where the Sunday afternoon ritual had started: toast and cocoa?—and when the numbers finally worked themselves out, he'd close the checkbook with a satisfied sigh. Then, the two of them would go into the living room and she'd settle herself on his lap and they'd watch whatever was on television, content just to be together.

Until being together became a bad thing, a time fraught with tension and anger and disappointment. Until Melanie told him she'd had enough, and she wanted him to leave. Although sometimes late at night, she wondered what was the final straw, and whether that straw had really been enough to break it all apart.

Carolee pursed her lips, erased the last two sets of numbers, recalculated the rest of them, and then handed the paper back to her father. She wanted it to be correct so they could put the book away and the two of them could go into the other room and just be alone for the little time remaining. Just half an hour, but even that was better than nothing. And next weekend she could spend two whole days with him.

"See, you did it!" Rob smiled at his daughter. "It just takes a little time. Sometimes you have to go back a few steps and start over, and then it all works out."

His words echoed in his mind. "Go back a few steps"— but it would take more than a few steps for him and Melanie. Miles before they could get back to the place where it was all good and they had plans for their future and then when she was pregnant, plans for the three of them.

Miles back and lots of detours that this time they would ignore: side roads they had mistakenly taken like the fight over the truck he had bought with what was left of their savings. Wrong turns like the time Melanie said—well, screamed, really, so loudly that she woke the baby—that she was sick of being poor and having to make do and couldn't he get a better job. The verbal roundabouts they would both be on during the worst of their fights, circling and circling with neither willing to give in or give up or do anything just to get off that endless loop of anger.

"Yay!" and Carolee quickly shoved the paper into her book and her book into her backpack before glancing up at the clock. It was quarter to five. There was only fifteen minutes before her father left. But that would be enough time to plan what they would do next weekend.

Saturday we could go to a movie, she thought. A movie, then back to his apartment where they could eat toasted cheese sandwiches with tomato soup. Then, on Sunday…

But before she could speak, before she could take him by the hand and go into the other room and talk about what they would do the next time they were together, her father stood up.

"Sweetie, it's getting late and I need to talk to your mother before I leave. So give me a hug and kiss and then why don't you go watch television or something."

Carolee knew what that meant. He wanted to be alone with her mother. He had something bad to say, something that would make her mother angry, and for just a minute she was angry too. Couldn't he just once not make trouble? If he made her mother angry, it would spill over to Carolee. And then late at night, she'd wake up and hear her mother crying, and bury her head under the pillow because she didn't know what to do and only wanted it all to stop.

But she couldn't change anything, couldn't stop the two of them from talking or fighting. So she gave him a hug and kiss, and then went up to her room, pausing on the bottom step in the hope that he would change his mind and call her back. But it didn't happen, so she continued on her way.

#

Rob heard her and knew by the way her footsteps sounded on the staircase that she was hurt and sad. But it had to be done, and squaring his shoulders, he turned to face Melanie.

"The plant closed down." The words came out harsher than he had intended and struck Melanie's face almost like a blow. "I didn't want to tell you. That's why I missed the last few visits. Plus, I've been looking for another job. But you know how it is. No one is hiring at the end of the year."

Melanie took a deep breath. Her first thought was the bills. How would she manage without what little money he sent her? And if he was out of work, then Carolee didn't have health insurance. What if she got sick?

She sat down heavily in the chair and buried her head in her hands, too upset and frightened to cry.

"That's why I haven't been around and because," here he swallowed hard, but decided to go ahead and tell her everything, "well, my landlord kicked me out and I had to move into a shelter. So, I can't take Carolee next weekend. As a matter of fact, I may have to miss the next couple visits. I need to save gas to go look for work. But it's not all bad news. One of the guys I work with—worked with," he corrected himself, "said that a plant in Braden is hiring but that's two hours away. I'm going there on Monday. If I get it, I'll let you know."

He took a deep breath. "I'll get something, Melanie. I promise," and he reached over to put a hand on her shoulder. "And it will all be okay."

She heard the note in his voice, the mix of hope and comfort, and for just a moment, let herself believe him. But only for a moment, and then it all came back: the disappointment, fear, anger, pain, regret—but regret for what? For ending their marriage or for marrying him in the first place? For encouraging him all the times when things didn't work out or for telling him it was all his fault: the lost jobs, the economic downturn, the reality that their life together didn't at all match the fantasy she had held onto?

She stood up, faced him, and took a deep breath, not knowing what she should say. And, with no words to express all that she felt, she reached out, picked up his empty coffee cup, and threw it against the kitchen door, where it shattered into pieces, a physical representation of what her marriage and life had become.

"Just go."

Only two words but behind them Rob heard all that she didn't say and knew that the distance between them was now even greater.

"I'm sorry." A futile response, but all he could manage through a throat constricted by emotion. He pulled on his coat and then opened the kitchen door, letting in a rush of frigid air. "Melanie?" One last word, a question really, but when no answer came, he left, closing the door behind him.

Melanie stood there, heart pounding, tears forming. She knew it wasn't all Rob's fault. She knew that other families faced the same situation. But it was easier to be angry with him than to admit to the fear that overwhelmed her. She walked over to pick up the shards of china, but when she reached the door, could only lean her head against it, listening for the sound of the truck's engine, hoping that he might come back and hold her and tell her it would all be okay and that she didn't have to deal with it all by herself.

But all she heard was silence.

#

He stepped off the porch and then paused to light a cigarette, one of two he allowed himself each day. He wasn't angry at Melanie, not really. He saw behind her reaction the fear and loneliness that clutched at her, the same emotions he faced each day, the same emotions that dogged his restless sleep.

He inhaled, held the smoke in his lungs, then released it, watching it drift upward through the falling snow.

Things will get better, and he wasn't sure if he was telling himself that or sending the thought to Melanie.

#

The sound of the cup crashing against the wall was so loud that Carolee heard it from the top of the staircase where she had been sitting, hoping until the last minute that her father might call her down and they could have just a little more time. Ten minutes, five even—that would have been enough.

But then Carolee heard the crash, followed by a silence that seemed to stretch forever, and finally the sound of the kitchen door shutting. She knew that he had left the house. She went into her room, pulling back the curtains to watch and hope. Maybe he had forgotten something in his truck and had just gone out to get it and then would come back into the house.

Maybe… But no. She saw his figure, shrouded in the darkness, pause on the walkway and then the brief flare of the match as he lit his cigarette. He wouldn't be coming back. Not tonight. Maybe not ever again. But she pushed that thought back into the dark corners of her mind.

Next week, she thought. He'll be back next week. And the week after that and maybe someday he won't ever leave.

#

Standing there in the frigid air, Rob finished his cigarette and then headed over to his truck. Would the engine start, allowing him to return to the life he had now? Or would the battery finally be so dead that the motor wouldn't turn over and he couldn't leave but would have to stay—go back through the door and into the kitchen, go back in time and into the life they once shared?

But when it did start, he gave one final glance at the house, at the kitchen door still shut, then up to the window where he thought he saw his daughter's outline.

Someday things will change, he thought as he shifted the truck into gear and backed down the driveway. If I can get the job and make enough money so Melanie wouldn't have to work so hard… If I can just make it all turn out right…

#

Melanie heard the truck engine catch, then the sound of the wheels crunching the ice and snow as Rob's truck made its way down the black-topped driveway. He was leaving, and she wasn't sure if she was glad that the fight was over or sorry that it had turned out that way again.

I don't understand, she thought wearily as she bent down to pick up the fragments of the cup. Where did we go wrong? Why did it have to turn out this way?

#

Carolee watched the truck slowly back down the driveway, and then the headlights flashed across the front of the house as he turned onto the street, the snowflakes glittering in their beam. She watched until he reached the corner and then turned again, watched until she couldn't see the truck anymore.

Then she slid open the window, heedless of the cold, listening for the sound of the engine. But all that came in on the wind was silence and the faint smell of burning tobacco, wending its way up to where she waited.

She breathed it in deeply, holding her father in her lungs, in her heart, never wanting to exhale again.

THE LANGUAGE OF LOVE

"Do you love me?"

The words rush out of me and the instant they are spoken, I want to recall them.

He sighs, a quick exhalation, and then frowns, before ruffling my hair.

"Next week, I'll change the oil in the car and tune it up, too. It probably needs it."

I need something, too, I want to say, but I don't. Instead, I murmur an assent, and give him a hug, hoping my question has not ruined our evening, wondering why I think it might.

"What should I make for dinner?"

"Anything. Anything that's easy," an apology, perhaps, for not saying what I want to hear: I love you with every bone in my body. Without you, my life is meaningless. You are everything to me.

"Your hair looks nice," he adds.

But I turn away without a response, unwilling to let him see how vulnerable I am to him, how even such a little bit of verbal caressing can make me weak.

"There's ground meat. Are tacos okay?" And the conversation shifts back to the prosaic topic of mealtime choices, away from the deep, dark waters that flood the heart.

When we first met, the words came fast between us: conversations lasting long into the night as we shared our thoughts and fears, hopes and dreams. The process of learning about each other was an exciting exploration. Each time we spoke, more strands from our past were woven into the present we were creating, intertwining the threads of our individual memories into a tapestry rich with shades and hues.

But years later, those vibrant colors had faded, and I couldn't recall the last time either of us had added a new strand, an unexpected thread.

Later: "Do you love me?"

I could be excused for asking this, lying as we are, legs and arms entangled, hearts beating in a counterpoint rhythm. I have to ask. I need to ask. I need to hear the words, so I can lay them in my memory, preserving them like the autumn's harvest, saving them for cold winters ahead.

The first time we came together, the excitement of the moment overshadowed any fears about the future. Two people overcome with passion, not thinking beyond the touch, the kiss, the split second between being two separate bodies and then one. And afterward, our quick inhalations gradually slowed down until we matched each other breath for breath. We laid there, skin to skin, throughout the long night, unwilling to allow even an infinitesimal space separate us.

But over the years, our need for that hours-long physical connection has ebbed. More often than not, a final kiss would signal the end of our lovemaking—still good and warm and wonderful even after all these years—before we would both turn away.

Tonight, he holds me close, saying just my name, his breath warm against my cheek. Then, as he rolls from the center of the bed to his side, "I noticed the faucet was leaking when you were washing dishes. I'll fix it tomorrow. A dripping faucet wastes water, you know."

I know that. And I know that water and gas and other natural resources should be conserved, husbanded, used judiciously, not squandered. But is emotion a natural resource? Is it possible to run out of love? Is that why he doesn't speak the words I long to hear? Or has the habit of not speaking overcome the need to talk, to share, to give voice to what is still felt deep in the heart?

The next day, he tackles the defective faucet. All morning long, he labors with the old pipes and rusted connections, swearing at the long-gone plumber, the manufacturer, the tool company that designed the wrench that keeps slipping.

Finally, he's done, and the faucet is repaired. I can see on his face that he's tired—but not too tired to stroke my shoulder in passing as he leaves the kitchen, carrying his toolbox. And I feel his touch long after he has left the room.

I suppose I will keep asking, hoping against hope that, one day, his defenses will be down, and he will say what I want to hear, need to hear.

Or has he been telling me all along, and I have not been listening?

LOVE DANCING

"Now let's have a toast for the happy couple! Many more years to both of you!"

My father smiles sheepishly as he rises to his feet, and then helps my mother from her chair. Together, they seem so old, so fragile. It's hard to believe that long ago their romance was fresh and new, that they were once passionately in love.

Like us. Like we are today. Will this be our tomorrow?

"And now, just for the two of you, a special song!"

My father gently embraces his bride of fifty years as the band begins to play an old favorite of theirs, and then, with a courtly bow, he asks her to dance. Amid applause and teary eyes, they glide on the floor, his arm around her waist, her small hand barely grazing his shoulder.

We watch them, my new love and I, and I wonder what he is thinking: How romantic? How corny? How soon can he decently leave this room where emotions lie in wait to snare the unwary?

We are too new to each other—I cannot read his mind. I know what he likes to eat, when he wants to make love, how long he will stay in the warm aftermath. But I don't know what he feels.

He is not a demonstrative man. In public, his gestures of affection are limited to brief hugs and briefer kisses. We have never even danced together.

Later, as I circulate among the guests with a tray of canapés, I hear my mother's voice.

"Joe and I have been very happy together. Oh, there have been problems," and I think back to the times when the silence between them was like January ice with no thaw in sight. Or when plates were set down on the table just a little too hard, doors shut just a little too firmly, voices pitched a little louder than usual. "But all in all, we have been happy."

My father is at the other end of the room, and as I drew nearer to him, I find he is talking not about his marriage but of the company he had left when he turned sixty-five. "The new men, now, they don't know a thing about troubleshooting. Back then, we put in a hard day's work, solving problems, and repairing equipment. Now, it's all replace, not repair. No one fixes anything anymore. They just get rid of it."

For a moment, I wonder if my father is talking about work or marriage. So many of my friends have been divorced. Were the relationships beyond repair? Or just beyond their ability to find the broken part and mend it?

I head back toward my mother, in time to hear a woman ask, "So, Mary, what's your secret for a happy marriage?"

My mother crinkles her forehead in concentration. "I don't know that there is a secret," she says thoughtfully. "You just do what you have to do, and later, when you look back, you see you made the right choice. If you're lucky," she adds honestly.

My lover finds me, as I stand there, caught by my mother's words. Is that what the secret is? I want to ask her. The secret is luck?

"Your tray is empty," he says, and I realize how silly I must look, standing still with an empty tray in my hands—a beggar child hoping for crumbs.

The band plays another song, a Glenn Miller melody that is a favorite of those who are old enough to remember when it was new, and gradually couples drift to the dance floor. I watch them, all these elderly, white-haired people, and envy them their history, the past that has brought them to this point—still together, still in love.

"You probably think this is silly, sentimental nonsense," I say finally, not looking at him, afraid of what I might not see.

He takes the tray from my hand and sets it down on a nearby table. Then, gently, he pulls me into his arms, and we sway together as the music plays.

THE MESSAGE IS UNDERSTOOD

"There isn't any more iced tea."

He stands in front of the open refrigerator door, as if by staring at the shelf he could magically make the pitcher appear, full to the brim. A statement of fact, but what he really is saying is please make some iced tea. The message is understood.

"Then make some," I want to answer, but instead I fill the pitcher with hot water, suspend five tea bags like mountain climbers dangling from thread ropes, and set it to steep on the counter.

This is how we ask each other to do things: no commands, just statements of fact that are interpreted by the other into requests for action. Even our decision to marry was not a clear-cut question-and-answer affair.

"My rent is going up next month," I had said. "And I'm hardly there anymore." *I don't want to live without you.*

"I don't have much closet space," he had answered. *I don't know if I can handle the responsibility of marriage. What if I fail?*

"You know, a house payment would be less than what we both pay in rent." *Give us a chance. Together we can do it.*

"I suppose it would be the practical solution. After all, other people manage." *There are happy marriages in this world. Maybe ours will be one, too.*

It has been two years now since we joined bodies, hearts, finances; two years of learning to hear what has not yet been spoken, of answering needs never admitted. The dialogue of marriage is a conversation on two levels: no demands, but expectations that the other will understand what should be done, what desires are awaiting fulfillment, what messages are sent without being spoken.

"The gas tank is empty," I say—my turn now.

He shakes his head but takes the keys, knowing how I hate to pump gas first thing in the morning. He will do this for me, the same way I will brew his morning coffee, because he hates to do anything before the caffeine enters his bloodstream.

This is how we settle small matters. But greater decisions take more time, more oblique references, more indirect observations.

"This is a beautiful cradle."

The auction was last fall, the contents of an old home now on the block—possessions of several generations given to strangers.

"Wouldn't it be lovely next to the fireplace?" By next Christmas, our child could be sleeping peacefully under a handmade quilt, while we string decorations on the tree.

"But our furniture is all chrome and glass," he had objected. "It wouldn't fit." A baby would mean a disruption in our lives, however welcome it would be. I don't know if I can handle that.

"Our furniture seems so cold. Perhaps we need to change our style," I answered, stroking the carved wood. *Maybe we need to change our life.*

We bought the cradle, but the chrome and glass furniture stayed—an uneasy alliance of style and desire, hopes and fears. Sometimes, when I dust, I set it swaying gently. Sometimes, when he lights the fire, I see him staring into its empty center.

While he is gone—filling the gas tank, checking the tires—the refrigerator stops humming and instead begins to rattle like a toy shaken by an angry toddler. An apartment-size model, it was old when we bought it, and now it is dying—on a hot July afternoon, with the freezer compartment full after last month's trip to the butcher shop.

By the time he comes back, I have the newspaper spread out before me, studying the ads on major appliances.

"The refrigerator is broken," I say.

He pulls out his tools, unwilling to surrender without a battle. Several hours later, he gives his verdict: "It can't be fixed. We need to buy a new one."

He comes over to the table to see the ads, but I have already turned the page. Pictures of baby furniture, baby clothes, baby toys lay spread out before us, and over the sound of melting ice, I hear my biological clock ticking.

"We have to buy a refrigerator," and gently, he takes the paper from my hands. *I know what you want, but I just don't know if I'm ready.*

At the store, we are overwhelmed with choices: side-by-side or freezer-on-top. Icemaker or door dispensers. Smoky black or pristine white. Too many options, too many decisions. He sees installment payments depleting the checkbook. I visualize children's drawings and school notes decorating the front.

"This looks like a good buy," I say. There is a shelf just the right size for baby bottles.

He looks at it doubtfully, reading the energy information, gauging the dimensions, and mentally comparing it with the one we have.

"It's much bigger than our old refrigerator." *Right now, there's just the two of us.*

"It doesn't pay to buy one too small. We have to think of the future." *A future with children in it. Isn't that what you want?*

He stands for a moment, thinking. Then, "Yes, we do," and he pays the bill.

The message is understood.

THE EQUATION OF LOVE

"We interrupt this program for breaking news. A commuter airplane has reportedly crashed during take-off—"

"Which airport?" My husband stands in the doorway, his suitcase in his hand. It's not a casual question nor one borne out of concern for the passengers. He simply wants to know if his own flight will be delayed.

I turn back to the set, in time to hear the newscaster say "...too early to speculate on the cause. However, flights out of the Warren airport are expected to be delayed only about one hour."

"One hour." He waits a moment, his forehead creased in thought. He is planning ways of using this time productively. My husband hates to have his plans disarranged or his time wasted. "I'd better go anyway. I can go over the figures for the meeting at the gate."

He comes over to kiss me good-bye, and then adds, almost as an afterthought, "I love you."

"Me, too," I answer, hearing the edge in my voice. Regretting it. I don't want to argue. At least, I don't think I do. Or I do, but don't want to lose the verbal battle.

"Listen, about last night—"

But I interrupt him. "I understand. It wasn't the right time. It wasn't safe." I hear the flatness in my voice and make an effort to smile. "Really. It's okay. We'll make love another time."

He looks at me, his expression inscrutable. For a moment, I think he might come back, kiss me one more time before leaving. But the moment passes. He switches his suitcase to his other hand, heads to the foyer and, his back to me, says, "Well, good-bye, then," before closing the door behind him.

News accounts that evening said the cause of the crash was still undetermined. There was no obvious reason for the failure. The plane had appeared in perfect working order—right up to the moment it crashed.

The next morning, I took my birth control pill. I had only one refill left before I needed to call my gynecologist for more. As I swallowed it, I wondered if this time next year, I'd still be taking them, or if I—we—might be trying to have a child.

"It's not the right time," my husband said last month. We were at Pizallo's—our favorite restaurant—celebrating our tenth anniversary. "We need to be in a better place financially."

And even though I didn't agree, I nodded.

My husband is an accountant. He works with facts, figures, financial statements. If it can't be itemized, computed, and neatly filed away, he doesn't want to deal with it. My longing for a baby has become a random number on the ledger—the journal difference that has thrown off the balance of our life.

I married my husband because I loved him. I still do. But it's difficult to restrict emotion to an easily defined formula. It's hard to keep desires within a set timetable.

"I need to be more established in my position," he had added, pouring more wine into our glasses. "When the time is right, we'll talk about it."

But the time hasn't been right for nearly five years now. And I wonder if the time will ever be right or if our chance will be gone.

I spend the next day vacuuming and cleaning—the unbroken Saturday routine. My husband's flight is due in by three in the afternoon. But by six-thirty, I have put away his unused dinner plate and cup, before pouring myself a glass of wine. And when he comes in the door at midnight, I am curled up on the couch, eating potato chips and watching an old movie.

"The meeting ran longer," he explains, hanging his suitcoat in the closet.

I think about offering him some coffee but decide not to move. Not yet.

"What are you watching?"

He isn't really interested in my viewing preference. He just wants to re-establish the lines of communication.

"Just an old movie," my eyes never leaving Ingrid Bergman's face as she says good-bye to Bogart.

"I don't want to fight with you."

His words surprise me. Usually, I am the one to make the first tentative gesture. I assume the blame for the problem, apologize for my emotions, make it all better again.

"But you have to understand—"

I get up before he can say anything else.

"I understand," and I walk past him. "The time isn't right. Someday we'll do it. Someday—" and my voice begins to shake. I am amazed at my reaction. I hadn't thought I was this angry, this hurt. "I'm going to bed now. I don't want to talk anymore."

I am still awake when he slides under the covers, sometime in the early hours of the morning. To my surprise, he slips his arm around me, curling his body against mine and reaching for my hand.

"There were twenty-five people on that plane."

I'm confused. Does he mean the plane he was on? Then I realize he is talking about the one that crashed.

"Twenty-three adults and two children." His breath stirs the hair at the nape of my neck. "Twenty-five people and they all died," and his voice held a wondering note in it, as though he couldn't quite believe the news.

My husband flies all the time. He has said that statistically planes are safer than cars. Numbers don't lie. But they don't save you either.

His arm tightens. "One of the passengers was the sales executive we were meeting with. His company was placing a major order, and he had some last-minute changes. But after the news broke, my boss called his office, and his assistant forwarded the needed information so we could make the changes. That's what took so long. But the deal went through," he adds flatly.

I don't know how to respond. With congratulations? With sympathy?

"I had met him last month at that sales convention in Tulsa. He and his wife just had a baby," he continues. "He showed me the pictures when we broke for lunch. They had been married ten years, and he had said that it seemed like now was the right time to start a family."

I hear the sharp intake of his breath and turn to face him, keeping hold of his hand. His fingers are cold, and I rub them gently, trying to warm them.

"I love you," he whispers. "I don't want to lose you. I don't want to lose our time."

I pull him against me and feel his heart racing. Gently, I stroke his back until, gradually, it slows to beat in time with mine.

LETTING GO

EARTH TO MOON

"Alice? Honey? What are you doing out there?"

Her husband's voice carried in the still evening air, calling to her, pulling at her.

"Nothing," she answered. Then amended her reply to "I was just throwing out the garbage."

She heard the door close, Richard satisfied for now with her response. These days, he had taken to keeping track of where she was, *how* she was. And she was fine. Really. Or if not fine, at least stable. Under control. Able to do daily tasks without stopping midway through, unsure of what she was doing or where she was. Or who she was. Or more precisely, who she wasn't. Not anymore.

Ignoring the trash bag on the ground, Alice watched as the sun moved closer to the horizon, the bands of orange and gold the last vestiges of life. Lately, she had taken on the after-dinner task of emptying the wastebasket and carrying the bag outside to the can. Not because she wanted to but because she felt almost compelled to check on the progress of the moon.

Was it coming back? Was it becoming bigger, fuller? When would it reach full moon—a beacon in the black sky sending a luminescent stream of light to connect it to the earth?

Last month (And was it only last month? Somehow, it seemed so much longer.) when Bethany started to lose her appetite, Alice looked for ways to entice her to eat. Late one evening, she held up the child so she could see the full moon from her hospital room window.

"Remember how the moon was just a tiny sliver in the sky?" and Bethany nodded slightly, her head a barely discernible weight against Alice's shoulder. "Now the moon is eating all its vegetables and drinking all its milk and it's growing big and strong! That's what you have to do!"

And for the next day or two, Bethany tried to nibble the food on her tray, giving Alice some hope.

"Don't you think she's looking better?" Alice had asked the oncologist then, while the two of them stood in the hallway. She glanced inside the room where Bethany lay propped up against the pillows. "She seems to have gained some weight. Her cheeks look fuller, don't they?"

And it was true. Bethany's face, once drawn like an old woman's, was rounder, plumper, reminding Alice of how she looked when she was an infant. When Bethany was little and baby fat creased her arms and legs and hid her cheekbones, Alice would call her "Little Moon Face" and then kiss her soft baby skin.

"It's the medication. It has that effect," the doctor answered, looking away as though he didn't want to see the impact his words were having on her. But he knew that the truth, in the end, was always better. "She's frail, and her last results were—" and there he paused, because there was no need to go on. Alice knew, as well as he did, what those results were, what they meant.

And if she needed further confirmation, it came as, day by day, Bethany's appetite faded, her round cheeks lost their fullness, and like the moon, she started to diminish.

"Sweetheart, I have to leave."

Startled, Alice realized Richard had come outside and was standing beside her. She hadn't heard the door open or his steps on the wooden porch.

"Alice?" He hesitantly touched her shoulder. "Will you be okay? I'll be back tomorrow around lunch. The meeting should only last a few hours and I've already booked my return flight."

She nodded, taking the bag over to the can and dropping it inside, then turned back to him. "I'll be fine. After all, it's just for one night. And I have plenty to do."

And she did. There were clothes to wash, furniture to be dusted, cards and letters to be answered. But once he drove away, she left those tasks uncompleted. Instead, she paced the floor, tracing the steps from their bedroom to the one that Bethany occupied—*had* occupied, she corrected herself—and then into the living room. And room by room, she turned on the lights, not wanting any space in the house to remain in darkness.

Bethany hated the darkness—*had* hated the darkness— and even at the hospital, Alice made sure the nurses understood that the bathroom light was to remain on all night long, the door ajar so the fluorescent gleam could filter into the room.

That was the first thing Alice did when she and her husband came home from the hospital just two weeks ago. (And had it only been two weeks? Somehow, it seemed so much longer.) Richard had gone inside to make the calls, but Alice remained on the porch, searching the cloudy sky for the moon. It was like looking at that first sonogram, when the technician had to point out where Bethany was in that sea of amniotic fluid that surrounded her.

But the new moon remained hidden, and she had finally given up. She went inside, where she began switching on every overhead light and table lamp in the house. And if Richard wondered why, he didn't ask.

It was a routine she had followed every night since then, even though she knew it made it harder for Richard to sleep in a room so brightly lit. It didn't bother Alice though, since she really wasn't sleeping anyway. In the middle of the night, she would sit by the living room window, tracking the shape and size of the moon. Two weeks ago, it was barely visible, then came the waxing crescent, followed last week by the first quarter, as the moon grew stronger, brighter, healthier.

She knew the moon's phases. She had watched them during all those long nights each time Bethany was admitted to the hospital. When Bethany was restless, Alice would make up stories about the moon, how the crescent moon hung an invisible bag of sunlight on its tip in case the sun grew hungry by the end of the day. How the moon wasn't gone during those few days after the last quarter but was only sleeping in the night sky, she told her daughter, "because it takes a lot of energy to shine so brightly."

How during the full moon, the light from the moon was a chute connecting it to the earth. "Like magic," she would tell Bethany. "And late at night, when everyone is sleeping, the stars take turns sliding down the beam just for fun. Like at a playground. Like you used to do. Like you'll do again when you're stronger."

But then, as the months passed and the hospital stays grew more frequent, Alice stopped telling that story because no one knew if Bethany would ever be that strong again. And during the last few weeks as the moon passed through its phases—the waning gibbous, then the third quarter—Bethany didn't want any stories. She would just lie in bed and stare out the window. And Alice would sit by her bedside and watch her daughter watch the moon.

By the time the orb had wasted away to its new moon stage, Bethany was gone, too.

The funeral was held the day after the moon entered its waxing crescent phase. A week later, when the moon reached first quarter size, she moved the sympathy cards from the dining room table to Bethany's room, slipping them into the dresser drawer next to her daughter's pajamas. And by the time the moon reached nearly three-quarters in size, Alice took to spending her evenings on the front porch watching it, waiting for it to grow to full size, suspended like a pearl in the evening sky.

That's where she was now. She had left the unfinished tasks behind and had come outside. The night sky was clear, no clouds marring the blackness, just the diamond glitter of stars.

Alice waited, and gradually the moon appeared over the tree line, round and bright, its light as translucent as Bethany's cheeks, as soft as Bethany's skin, as fragile as Bethany's life. And as she watched, the glow of the moon grew stronger, cutting through the darkness of pain and connecting the grieving mother to her lost daughter with the indestructible light of love.

GOODBYES

THE TRICYCLE

"How much for the tricycle?"

The driver, a roughly dressed bear of a man, had pulled up as she had finished setting out her garage sale items: the odds and ends that she wasn't taking to the much smaller apartment, the items that were no longer a good fit for her much smaller family.

She took a step back to put some distance from him. He unnerved her. He was so big, and she was alone, except for her daughter.

Before she answered, Carla glanced over at Hayley who was immersed in arranging a set of expensive saucepans in a row, shortest to the tallest. Jason had bought them last year when he decided to take up gourmet cooking: one of many interests that were destined to be forgotten after a period of time.

Like parenting. Like marriage.

"How much?" he repeated impatiently.

She answered in a lowered tone, "Five dollars," adding, in case he wondered why it was so cheap, "My daughter got a two-wheeler for her birthday, and she doesn't need this one anymore," wondering if that was really the case or just what she told herself.

It was true that Hayley received the new bike for her birthday last week, one of several gifts that Carla gave her that had a double intent: as a present for turning five but also as an enticement to help her adjust to the changing circumstances. But when she proposed adding the tricycle to the list of items for sale, her daughter resisted.

"No!" holding tightly to the handlebars of her beloved three-wheeler she had named Annabelle until her knuckles turned white.

"There's not enough room in the apartment entryway for two bikes," Carla had explained, but Hayley shook her head, not letting go.

But no matter how hard you held onto something, thought Carla as she left the room, you couldn't stop it from being taken from you. Like her dream of a family: two people who loved each other and who together would love their daughter.

Trying again last night, Carla said, "There's a park across the street from our new place and I saw lots of other kids your age riding bikes there. Two-wheelers, like your new one!"

But Hayley, mute, only frowned before wheeling the tricycle up the hall to her bedroom.

Carla let it go. It had been a long day of packing, and she was tired and not up to any more arguments about what goes and what stays—a variation of those conversations she had had with Jason until the last and final one. The only difference was the pronoun: not "what" but "who"—who is going and who is being left behind.

The next morning, as Hayley stood in front of her tricycle, trying unsuccessfully to shelter it from her mother, Carla used her last line of reasoning, hating herself for doing so.

"You don't want those kids to think you're a baby, do you? They'll laugh at you! You're too big for a tricycle anyway!"

Reluctantly, her daughter let it go, and Carla carried it out to the small lawn to join the other ticketed items. But now, with a prospective buyer standing before her, she wondered if it was the right move, if anything she was doing was the best for Hayley.

"Okay, here" and the man handed over five creased one-dollar bills that Carla hurriedly slipped into the pocket of her jeans.

He took the tricycle to his battered pick-up truck, emblazoned with Jonah's Junk Collection on the side, and tossed it into the bed where it bounced off the corner of an old washing machine before landing atop a stack of metal shelves.

The noise drew Hayley's attention, and she came rushing over.

"You're hurting Annabelle!" she cried, tugging at his sleeve. "You shouldn't throw her like that! She'll get all scratched!"

Eyebrows raised, he looked down at her and then over at Carla.

"It's what she named it," she explained, and then shrugged, hoping that he would drive away and put an end to it, wondering if it had been a mistake to give her the other bike now. Maybe she should have waited until after the move or allowed her to keep them both. But it was too late now.

Too late, and now Hayley was crying. "I want to see Annabelle! I want to say goodbye!"

Carla moved to pull her daughter away, but then stopped as the man lifted the tricycle from the bed of the truck and set it on the grass in front of them.

"You're right," he said gently. "I shouldn't have done that. She's a good bike and she'll make some other little girl—someone much smaller than you—very happy. You tell her that and then say goodbye. Okay?"

Hayley reached out and stroked the scratched fender, and then ran her hand lovingly over the handlebars. "Bye-bye, Annabelle," she whispered. "I won't forget you."

Then she stepped away and nodded to the man, who, Carla realized, didn't seem all that big and threatening any more.

He patted Hayley on the head, then picked up the tricycle. But instead of putting it back in the bed, he opened the passenger door and set it on the seat.

"There," he said, turning the handlebars so it seemed to be looking out the window. "Now she can look where she's going."

He smiled at Hayley, then got into his truck and drove away, leaving Carla and her daughter standing in the driveway. Hayley shouted, "Bye-bye, Annabelle!" as she waved until the truck disappeared around the corner.

"She'll be happy, right, Mommy? She'll be okay in her new home, won't she?"

And as Carla nodded, she knew the question wasn't only about the tricycle but for them, too.

"Yes. She'll be just fine. Everything will be okay."

#

IN THE SPRING

The sun was setting, taking with it what little warmth it gave, and Jenny shivered a bit as she took the last bulb from the netted sack. But the old woman was determined to get the crocuses planted before the November weather turned cold and unforgiving.

She would have liked to have done it a few weeks ago when the temperature was warmer, but she had to wait for Jackson, the grounds manager of the assisted living facility, to give her permission. She had to ask permission for everything:

to change the curtain rod in her small living quarters, to put a sign outside her door that said "Please knock" so aides wouldn't enter unexpectedly, even to move the rocker she had brought from home closer to the window.

At least her room *had* a window. Some of the others didn't or looked out over the asphalt parking lot. But hers faced south into the courtyard, and there were trees where birds made nests, and one small plot where a few rosebushes had bloomed half-heartedly in the summer sun. That's what gave her the idea. She could picture how that small square of dirt would look in the spring when crocuses would push their way through the half-frozen surface inch by inch, and then confidently open their delicately-petaled flowers to the sun.

"I'll buy the bulbs and plant them myself. You won't have to do anything," she said to Jackson, the words reminding her of what her son used to say when he tried to talk her into letting him have a puppy.

And something in her tone or the look in her eyes had softened the man. He wiped his hands on his overalls and then said, sighing as though he knew this would someday be his responsibility, "Okay, fine but only in that space. And don't tell anybody that you're doing it, or I'll have everyone asking for their own flowerbed!"

Jenny was surprised. She hadn't expected him to give way but now that he had, she could focus all her thoughts on the bulbs she would buy: what colors she would choose and how she would arrange them. Perhaps by shade: lavender first, followed by yellow, then cream, with white at the very edge. Or mix them all together: a mosaic of soft colors that spoke of the delicacy of the season, of life itself.

Over the long weeks of the summer, as the drug slowly dripped down the narrow tube into her vein and the radiation burned away what was left inside, she kept the image of the flowering crocuses firmly in her mind. And if at times she worried that she might not be up to the task—that she wouldn't be strong enough, well enough, to plant all the bulbs she ordered—she would push those thoughts from her consciousness.

When autumn came and it was time, Jenny was ready. She had her brand-new trowel and a ruler to mark the depth of the holes, and a stack of Sunday newspapers she had saved to provide some cushioning for her knees. It took her several weeks to get all the bulbs into their new home, partly because of the fall rains and partly because of the energy it required from her. A half-hour of planting meant several days of rest before she could go out again.

But Jenny was determined, and now her determination had paid off.

She got to her feet, not without some difficulty after being in that position for close to an hour, and gave the bed one final look. The bulbs were in, and the mulch smoothed back over the soil.

"Goodbye for now, but I'll see you all next spring," she said softly.

Next spring—when the bed would be filled with a collage of color, welcome after the dark cold winter.

Next spring—when she would be strong enough, well enough, to sit outside and enjoy their beauty.

Next spring…

#

BETWEEN THE LINES

The first indication came nearly seven months after he had been deployed. A letter from his wife, nearly two pages long, starting with a question about his health and well-being, followed by details about the various household tasks she had undertaken: tires rotated, furnace air filter replaced, lawn furniture stored away.

Then the brief postscript, added almost as an afterthought below her name: "Paul, my new boss, asked me if I wanted to be his executive assistant. More hours, but more money. I'll let you know what I decide."

Not "What do you think?" Not "I'll take it just until you come home." Not "This means we can buy a bigger house and have a baby and live happily ever after."

No, merely "I'll let you know what I decide" as though her decision didn't affect both of them, as though she was just a friend or co-worker, rather than his wife of five years—six, come September.

The next letter, barely a page, came a month later, sent on to the base where he had been transferred. It was less about the house and more about her work: the people she had lunch with, the new client projects she was handling. And then, "My promotion was approved, but I've had to work late three nights a week. Paul said it's important that I get up to speed on my new responsibilities."

The third was even shorter, as though she had dashed it off in between phone calls. "Paul said"—and how he hated the way she wrote "Paul said"—"now that I'm his assistant, I'll be attending the quarterly meeting next month with him at the home office. It's a three-day event, but the company pays for everything: transportation, food, the hotel."

He thought about writing to her, saying how much he loved her, missed her, how he couldn't wait until he was stateside again. Hinting (in carefully worded phrases so the censors wouldn't black them out) that he was moving closer to the action, to the fighting, and how the thought of her, of their marriage, was the single thing that kept him going. Reminding her of the plans they had made so long ago, of the children they wanted to have, of the future they wanted to create.

But he didn't because, after all, what was the point?

He tucked the letter in with the others in the side pocket of his duffle bag and then waited for his orders. He couldn't tell her where he was going or for how long he'd be gone. She might not even know that he had moved from base to base, since the letters were forwarded.

And by the time the next letter came, the one where she started off saying how much she still loved him and ended with "I never meant to hurt you, you know. Goodbye," it didn't matter anymore.

THINKING ABOUT MELANIE

It's so cold outside that, when I breathe, the air is razor-sharp against my throat and lungs. I ought to stay inside but it's my first chance to be outdoors in the past two weeks, and I feel the need to escape from all those well-meaning people.

Too much sympathy can weaken the soul.

"Have some coffee, dear." "Are you warm enough?" "Have you been sleeping any better?"

Countless questions and they all have my best interests at heart—more than I do, in fact. It's just that none of it seems all that important anymore—not meals or drinks or sleep. Not since Melanie—but I'm not going to think about Melanie today.

Anyway, the walk will do me good. It's almost half a mile—past the house and down the long hill leading to the schoolyard. Tomorrow, if the snow comes as the weatherman has promised, the hill will be covered with children on sleds of all types and sizes, fighting for a chance to ride headlong into the whiteness, only to tumble off their seats in the end.

The ride itself is over in seconds, and then the children must face the long trudge up the hill, just to enjoy a brief thrill before they fall again. But they never grow tired of it.

Perhaps, being children, they don't see the connection between sledding and real life—quick thrills followed by predictable falls and endless climbs back up hills that grow harder and higher each time.

Melanie used to sled ride, too. But she always chose the part of the slope with the least incline, and further delayed the end by dragging her red boots off the side. She never wanted the ride to be over.

But there—I said I wouldn't think about her today. Not about the way her cheeks would blush scarlet in the frosty air or the way her blonde curls would stream out behind her or the way her hands—in red mittens matching her boots— would grip the rope of the sled so tightly I would have to pry her fingers free.

And in the end, that's what I had to do. She had gripped my hand so tightly that, when it was over, I had to loosen her fingers one by one before I could free myself. And it was the hardest thing I had ever done.

But enough of that. No one wants to hear about it anymore. They just keep saying all the same things over and over: "Just thank God she wasn't sick a long time." Or "Remember the good times, my dear, and be grateful for them, at least." Or, the worst one yet: "As time passes, your wounds will heal, and you can start life over again."

Why does everyone think I want to feel better? If I thought for one minute there was any chance of the pain easing, I would pick and pull at the scab until it bled again. I'd rather endure the agonizing pain that comes with remembering Melanie than stop hurting and forget her.

Not that I think there's much chance of that ever happening.

The hill is very slippery, the dead grass ice-encrusted. I'd better concentrate on walking one step at a time until I reach the bottom. Everything is icy—the bare branches of the oaks, the cement sidewalks, the black asphalt streets. Parents have been warning their children to be extra careful at the intersections, just in case the cars can't stop on the glassy roadway in time.

All too often, you know, there isn't enough time. We have all been lulled into believing that tomorrow or the next day or the next week there will be time to do all the things we promised ourselves and our children we would do.

"Later," we say, "Mommy's busy now. We can do it when there's more time."

But sometimes, there just isn't any more time. And then, all the gripping of hands and crying of tears won't give you one more minute.

"The moving finger writes; and having writ, moves on: Nor all thy piety nor wit shall lure it back to cancel half a line, nor all thy tears wash out a word of it."

I think that's how the quote goes—from *The Rubaiyat of Omar Khayyam*, I believe. It was part of the opening sequence of *The Flying Dutchman*—a movie I vaguely recall catching on television late one night. It was one of those long nights when Melanie had colic, and all I wanted to do was sleep but all she wanted to do was cry.

"What's wrong with you?" I remember saying. Or screaming, more likely. Not to excuse myself, but I was young and alone and new to motherhood. And short on sleep and patience and understanding.

Anyway, I screamed and she cried, and then I cried, and finally, I think we both sobbed ourselves to sleep sometime around four in the morning.

It's hard to believe that, once, the only thing I wanted was for Melanie to fall asleep and give me some time alone.

I've reached the bottom of the hill now, without even falling. Not much of an achievement to be proud of, but it's the best I can do these days. I used to think the worst thing in life would be to lose my job or fall prey to some nameless illness rendering me incapable of caring for my child.

And when I would be in the middle of yet another love affair, I would think that, when he left me (and they always left me) it would be absolutely the worst thing that could happen.

But now, the worst has undeniably occurred, and in a strange way, it has liberated me from all those fears. After all, you can only die once—the essential you, that is. You might continue to walk around, talking and laughing and breathing, but you are still dead inside.

And you realize it doesn't matter any longer what else might happen. After all, the worst has already claimed you. Anything else would be anti-climactic.

Here, at the bottom of the long, curved driveway in front of the school, the buses have already begun to line up. Because we live so close, Melanie never rode the bus. Instead, I would walk to meet her, sometimes bringing her an apple or banana to snack on during the walk home.

On payday, as a special treat, we would stop at the corner bakeshop to choose a pie for dinner. Melanie liked apple pies with snowdrifts of whipped cream piled high. I used to tell her too much whipped cream would make her sick. Now, I would buy it by the gallon and let her take her chances.

It's getting late. I ought to head back home where someone is sure to be waiting. There's been an unofficial sign-up sheet circulated among the neighbors to make sure I'm not left alone one minute more than necessary.

People bring me dinner, take me out for lunch, stop by for morning coffee. The only time they can't cover is night. Then, they have their own lives to attend to—children to tuck in and husbands to hold.

What they don't understand is that I don't mind being alone. It gives me a chance to walk through the empty rooms, seeing Melanie everywhere, straining for the echoes of her voice, willing myself not to forget.

Almost 3 p.m., and the children are nearly through for the day. From my vantage point outside the school windows, I can see them, learning arithmetic number by number. Except, as Melanie used to correct me, it's "not arithmetic, Mommy. It's called math."

But it looks the same to me. One plus one still equals two—no matter what you call the process.

Only now, I do a different kind of sum in my head. One plus one will always equal two, but two take-away one equals nothing—emptiness—zero.

Two minus one is Melanie gone.

SEEING JIM

"Jim? Are you awake? I want to read you something."

Carol looked over at her husband, and although his eyes remained closed, the brief movement of his head indicated that he was listening.

So, she continued. "'Small cottage on lakefront, three bedrooms, two baths, half-acre property with fruit trees.'" She raised her head to glance at him. "It sounds just like what we always wanted. Just think, in the summer you can fish, and I can take care of the garden, and in the fall we can pick apples and pears and—"

But there she stopped because her husband's steady breathing and almost imperceptible snore told her he had fallen asleep.

He had been sleeping a lot these past few weeks. Carol had hoped that the last surgery would make him stronger, more alert, more aware, even though the surgeon had advised her repeatedly against such unfounded optimism.

"Right now," he had told her bluntly last week while Jim was in the recovery room, "our goal is just to get him back to the nursing home."

But Carol wanted more than that, and at first, the operation did seem to have made a difference. Once his oxygen levels had improved to the point where all he needed was the nasal cannula rather than the face mask, he was discharged back to the care facility. As for his appetite, some days he even ate almost half of his meals, Carol carefully documenting what and how much he consumed.

Each change became another step to what she viewed as Jim's journey back to their home, even though when she broached the idea, the nursing home doctor shook his head.

"He requires more than you can provide, unless you have round-the-clock nursing care. It's better if he stays here so he can get the kind of medical attention he needs."

Reluctantly Carol had agreed, thinking to herself, *only for now*. She was sure that in another few weeks—at worst, a few months—Jim would have regained enough strength and energy so that she could bring him back to their house. And then, after a little more time, they could even go for drives out to the country as they used to. They had spent so many Sundays traveling to rural villages and farming communities, looking for places where they could move now that Jim had retired.

"A nice little cottage in the country," he had said—Was it just a few months ago? She couldn't remember. "We'll use the money we get for this place and still have plenty left. What do you think?"

She had agreed, and so each Sunday morning she would pack the small cooler with snacks and drinks for their day's journey to unfamiliar places in search of their future home.

That's what their plans were the day it happened. They were going to see a small bungalow once Jim came back from the hardware store where he was buying a few pieces for the leaking bathroom faucet. It was one of the many tasks on the to-do list that he was working through in preparation for putting their house up for sale.

And when her cell phone rang and she saw his number on the caller ID, she thought perhaps he needed more information to be sure he was buying the correct part.

But it wasn't Jim. It was someone at the hospital who had found his phone among his bloodstained clothing, had scrolled through the contact list until locating one that said "Carol—wife" and had made the call. By the time she reached the emergency room, Jim's pressure and heart rate were dropping, and the doctor told her gently that even if the surgery worked, he might not make it through the night.

She had sat there through the interminable hours as the surgeons tried to put his broken bones and damaged organs back into some semblance of correctness. And while she waited, she wondered why that truck driver hadn't seen her husband crossing the parking lot and whether Jim would ever forget the feel of the impact of the vehicle crashing into his body.

From that day forward, Carol was on a different type of journey, one that she felt ill equipped to take. But unlike the highway signs and mile markers that would lead to those long-ago destinations, the endpoint for this trip was unknown, with the route they were following indicated only by a series of notes Carol made in her journal as she tracked Jim's progress: *The surgical site on his spine shows improvement. The pulse in his left foot is weaker. He's gained a half pound. He's lost some feeling in his right arm. They've taken him back to the hospital. He's been discharged back to the nursing home.*

Gains, then losses. Better, then worse. Richer or poorer, as the wedding vows went. And that too was a facet of her life: each evening, struggling to figure out how to pay the ever-mounting balances on medical bills. But each day, from six in the morning until he was given his last medication at midnight, she tried her best to put those worries aside and talk about the future—a future, she told herself, that she and Jim still had, a future that she could almost see, one with the two of them together.

"This house," pitching her voice slightly louder so if Jim was awake he could hear her, but not enough to disturb him if he was sleeping, "is well within our budget. We can sell our home and buy this one and be in it before fall. Just in time to pick the fruit from the trees."

She kept talking even though she knew he wasn't listening. "I think somewhere I have my mother's recipe for cinnamon-clove applesauce. I'll buy some canning jars and make enough to last all winter."

"How is he doing today?"

The sound of Rafael's voice startled Carol. She hadn't heard the aide come in. For a large man, he was very quiet in both movement and demeanor.

"Fine," she said. "Better," she added, not that there was any indication of improvement. Quite the opposite, in fact. But it was what she told herself, *had* to tell herself.

Rafael nodded. "I was going to give him a sponge bath, but I hate to disturb him," he said. "Why don't I come back in a bit?"

Carol nodded and with one final glance at her, Rafael left the room. She wondered if he had heard any of the one-sided conversation, and if so, if he would mention it to anyone on the staff. When Jim was first brought to the nursing home, the social worker had done her best to prepare Carol for what she termed the realities of the situation.

But Carol persisted in her belief that it was just one way of looking at it. The other was that Jim would defy the odds: heal faster, get better, regain his abilities until he was back to being the man she knew, the husband she needed and wanted and loved. That was what she held onto all those long days in the hospital, and what sustained her once they moved him here. She had to. It was all she had left.

In the early days right after he had arrived, Carol had talked to the staff doctor about the possibility of taking Jim out for short drives once he was stronger.

"Just so he could see something other than these four walls," she had explained. "Not now, of course, but in a month or two. Maybe if he was out for a while, he would improve, be more, I don't know…" And she stopped because what she wanted to say was, be stronger, healthier, not teetering on the edge.

Perhaps recognizing that Carol, like so many family members he talked with, needed something to sustain her, the doctor had simply responded, "We'll see how it goes"—an answer that, if unsatisfactory, was better than a flat-out negative.

So, during the next few weeks, she had made endless notes, looking for any signs that progress was being made. Although the truth was Jim never seemed to feel any better, be any better. All he did was grow smaller and weaker and more frail right before her eyes. But Carol wasn't ready to give up, give in. Instead, she would spend the long hours when he was sleeping—and lately it seemed he was always sleeping— reading real estate ads in search of the home the two of them would occupy when he was better.

Not *if*, she would tell herself when doubt crept into her mind, but *when*. When he was better. When their life returned to the way it once was and their future again held possibilities.

Jim stirred a little and Carol resumed the conversation.

"Think about it, Jim. Fresh air and sunshine and homegrown vegetables. How much—" and she almost said "healthier" but stopped herself. That was a word that she tried not to use when talking to Jim or about Jim—"how much quieter it would be there! Just the sounds of the birds in the morning and the frogs at night. Would there be frogs, I wonder? There must be because there is a lake, and frogs like being by the water. I read somewhere that they hide out in the reeds that grow on the edge of ponds and streams."

She was rambling. She knew it. Knew, too, that Jim wasn't listening, that he had once again fallen asleep or what passed for sleep these days. He was somewhere else, away from his body and all the pain that tormented him, leaving her behind.

"I was thinking that I should go and take pictures and then, when I come back, I'll tell you all about it. And when you're—" and she almost said "stronger" but that was another word that she didn't use when talking to Jim or about Jim—"ready, we can go together, and you can decide."

That was a formality. Jim had long since stopped making any decisions for the two of them. He left that to her.

She set the newspaper on the foot of his bed and closed her eyes. She didn't know why she was so tired all the time. It wasn't as though she was doing anything. All she did was sit and watch Jim sleep. Or when he was awake, she would talk to him or feed him his meals or gently massage lotion on his arms and legs the way the physical therapist had showed her. There wasn't much else she could do.

"Ma'am? I thought I'd do his bath now, before the lunch trays arrive. That might perk him up, so he'll eat a bit more."

Carol opened her eyes and looked up at Rafael. He had been a godsend when they first arrived, and she was glad that he had been assigned to care for Jim: to change his gown and bathe his body. Carol could never have done it. Even in his weakened condition, Jim was too heavy for her to manage. But Rafael, a muscular man with strong hands and kind eyes and a soft voice, could do it all with a minimum of movement. Sometimes, she thought her husband fell asleep during the process, lulled by the soothing motions of the soft washcloth against his skin and the warm water washing away the sweat from his body.

She moved to pick up the newspaper, but Rafael reached over and handed it to her, glancing first at the open section.

"House-hunting again," she explained, and he nodded. She had told him about their plans, and if he knew that it would never happen, he didn't dispute her goal but simply listened. "I found one that Jim would have—that Jim would like," hoping he hadn't caught her speaking in the past tense about her husband who was still here. "There's an open house this afternoon and it's such a nice day for a drive…" her voice trailing off.

"Why don't you go?" he suggested. "I'll wash him up and give him his lunch, and afterward the physical therapist will be in to do his exercises. You usually take your break then anyway."

Her "break," as Rafael called it, was when she sat in the cafeteria, picking at whatever was on the menu that day, instead of being in the room while the therapist did whatever she had to do to try to stimulate Jim's muscles and tendons and nerves. Carol couldn't bear to be in there while the session took place, not after the first one when the slightest movement brought tears to her husband's eyes and to hers as well.

She knew it had to be done, and the therapist was as gentle as possible, but still it was too much for her to watch.

"You need to get out for a while," Rafael said encouragingly. "It's important that you don't spend all your time here in this room, you know."

Carol nodded. Rafael was right. The social worker had told her the same thing when she came in one morning during the first few days to find Carol still there, having slept all night in the easy chair.

"You must go home at night," she had said gently but firmly. "The staff will keep an eye on your husband and call you if anything changes"—Carol knew what that meant, since they would hardly call her if Jim was improving—"but it's important that you take care of yourself."

From that day forward, Carol spent her nights alone at home, carefully keeping to her side of the bed as though Jim was still there, her cell phone on the nightstand with the ringer turned up, so she would hear the sound no matter how deeply she was sleeping. Not that she ever slept all that well those nights. Instead, she catnapped away the hours until it was time to shower, dress, and go back to Jim's bedside.

That's where she spent every day. It became a new normal, a new way of living. But something about the description of that lakeside cottage called to her, and she thought perhaps she could go, should go, and see what it was like. Rafael was right. It would do her good to get out of this room, this place, if only for a few hours.

Not that she wanted to get away from Jim. What she wanted was to get away from what was happening and then come back to the life they had planned rather than the life they were living. To think of something other than blood tests and CT scans and medications and all that came with it.

"There's no need to hurry back. We'll take care of things here," Rafael added as he filled the basin with warm soapy water to bathe Jim. "Go look at the place, have a meal in a restaurant, enjoy the fresh air. It's a beautiful day, you know."

And she noticed with surprise that he was right, that the sun was shining and the leaves on the trees were gently moving in the soft spring breeze.

"I'll only call you if…" and he stopped there.

But she knew what he meant. If something went wrong. If Jim took a turn for the worse. If they had to call for an ambulance. If, if, if… the conjunction was a constant presence in every conversation, like the hum of the oxygen machine or the beeping of the bedside monitor.

"Go on now," he said, like a parent to a reluctant child.

Carol obeyed, stopping first to kiss Jim on the cheek. "I'll be back in a bit and then I'll tell you all about it and show you the pictures and you can tell me what you think. It might be just what we need, Jim—a fresh start."

But there was no response. Sighing, she picked up her purse and jacket from the other chair, and then, with a final glance at her sleeping husband, left the room.

Rafael was right. It was a beautiful day. Carol rolled down the car window just enough to feel the breeze on her face. She had forgotten how fresh air smelled and how the songs of the birds sounded. And as she drove along the highway, she breathed it all in deeply, trying not to feel guilty about being outside when Jim was inside.

"Just a few more weeks," she said aloud, "and then he can be going for drives with me."

And if her voice held no conviction, she ignored it. She had gotten very good at ignoring what she didn't want to hear or see. It was the only way she could get through the days and nights.

The directions were simple: take Interstate 11 until she reached exit 23, and then turn right on County Line Road and then right again on Old Mill Lane. Then follow it until she arrived at the house, just beyond the small town, less than forty miles away from the hospital but seemingly in another world.

When she reached the house with its For Sale sign leaning against the maple tree at the edge of the long drive, she saw immediately that the advertisement, while accurate, had failed to do the home justice. It was a lovely home, a welcoming home, the kind of home they had been looking for.

It's perfect, she told herself, seeing how the sun had moved over the roofline to bathe the back of the east-facing house. If we slept in the front bedroom, Jim would wake to the morning light. And there was plenty of space for a small garden. I could grow our own vegetables and that would be so much better for both of us.

Carol left the car and started photographing the house: the big front porch with the swing where she could see Jim resting after lunch, and the back patio just off the kitchen where the two of them could have their evening coffee. And the bay window in what must be the living room… That's where she would place the Christmas tree with all its lights and decorations, she decided.

She took picture after picture, all the while imagining the life she and Jim would have in this place. A wonderful life. A long life.

And when her cell phone rang and the caller ID told her it was Rafael, she ignored it and kept taking more pictures, seeing Jim on the porch, on the patio, seeing Jim in the window, at the door… seeing Jim…

LOVE LETTERS

January 1

Sweetheart,

The new year started with a blizzard. Not that it was any surprise. For the past two days, the weather forecast had been full of warnings about excessive snowfall. Fortunately, Abel stopped by with his snowblower and cleared the drive. Otherwise, I would have been stuck here for days, since when the city's snowplow cleared the road, it left a wall of icy whiteness at the bottom of the drive.

This is the kind of weather you always enjoyed: an expanse of white with only deer and rabbit tracks marring the surface. If you were here, you would be outside, filling the bird feeders and suet cages for the chickadees and cardinals and stuffing the wooden holder with corncobs for the squirrels. And then you would bring in armloads of kindling for the wood stove and settle yourself in front of it with a cup of coffee and the newspaper, reading headlines to me while I made dinner.

Instead, I'm watching the snow come down, and trying to ignore the plaintive cries of the birds and the insistent chatter of the squirrels—all of whom want me to come out and take care of their needs.

But it's too cold to go outside. Or perhaps I don't want to take over what was once your role. I've done enough of that the past month.

#

February 14

Sweetheart,

I was thinking of the first Valentine's Day we spent together. We'd only been dating a month or so, and I wasn't sure where our relationship was going. Or, for that matter, if I even wanted it to go anywhere. I'd been hurt in the past when I let my hopes get too high for a new lover only to have them dashed in the end. It seemed like a much better idea to keep what had started between us on a platonic level.

But you had other intentions, and when you arrived on that Valentine's Day, you had an armload of scarlet red roses, a three-pound box of dark chocolates tied with a golden ribbon, and an invitation to dine at the best restaurant in town.

Of course I said yes—what girl wouldn't? But it was a qualified yes, one that came with no promises.

It took you a year to break down my defenses and tear down the walls I had built. A year for me to see that you were different, that our relationship could be different, that a future with you was infinitely better than a life alone.

I'll never understand why you kept trying, why you never gave up. But I am glad you did, even now.

#

March 20

Sweetheart,

The weather has been unseasonably warm, and today, perhaps to celebrate the first day of spring, the crocuses made their appearance. Their delicate blooms of purple and yellow and white stood out in sharp contrast against the mud and muck left by melting snow. But more snow is predicted by the weekend, so I'm not certain how well they will fare. Perhaps they are stronger than I believe, despite their fragile appearance. I hope so.

Sonia called the other day. She said she was going to the nursery to order some plants and asked if I wanted to go along for the ride, although I suspect it was just to check on me. You should be very proud of your daughter. She stops by at least once a week and has invited me over for dinner at least two or three times a month, even though she is so busy with work and the twins. Max has been working long hours at his business, and I gather from the little Sonia has mentioned that things are not going well at the company, and she's concerned about her husband.

I'm meeting with our accountant next month to see what shape our finances are in. I hope there's enough that I can help pay for our grandsons' tuition. I hate to see Sonia and Max worry so much. I know how money woes can affect a marriage.

#

April 1

I found it. After all these years, after everything we have been through, after everything *I've* been through the past five months, and now this!

How appropriate that it occurred today, on April Fool's Day. I guess for all those years I was the fool.

Why did you keep that letter? Why didn't you tear it up, throw it in the trash, burn it in that damn wood stove you so loved?

No, you kept it. And there it was, shoved behind the folders that held the financial paperwork from previous years. And I never would have known it was there except that Bill reminded me to bring last year's records when we meet to finish the taxes. Something about reviewing the investments and projecting what our—my—future needs will be.

Oh, hell, what does it matter why I was going through the file drawer? What matters is that I found it, in the envelope that was addressed to you and mailed to your office—probably because she was afraid I might open it if it came to the house.

And I would have. You had been so distant, so quiet for several months. But every time I asked you what was wrong, you gave me some vague answer about work worries. And that was the year when Ben had all those ear infections and needed to have tubes inserted, and Sonia had broken her leg playing soccer, and it was all I could do to stay on top of their doctor's visits and schoolwork.

And by the time you told me, several weeks after you said you had ended it, I was so exhausted from caring for the children that I couldn't even process it.

You said you were sorry. You said it was over. You said— well, it doesn't even matter what you said. All I knew was that I had two choices: stay or leave. I stayed. And you swore you'd make it up to me and I believed you.

But in her letter, she wrote that she understood why you made the decision to remain married, and that she respected you for doing your duty. Your duty? Was that what I was to you? A duty that you had to fulfill? An obligation that you had to honor?

All this time I thought you stayed with me, stayed in our marriage, out of love. Now I wonder.

#

May 25

Ben was in town on a business trip, and he and Sonia took me out for dinner. The children must have remembered it would have been our fiftieth wedding anniversary and I suppose they didn't want me to spend it alone. Little did they know that the last thing I wanted to think about was our marriage. Every time I recall the words she used in that letter, so many emotions overwhelm me. Anger, sadness, bitterness—you name it and I have felt it.

Although, if I'm going to be honest (and I might as well be at this point), there is also a trace of self-recrimination. Yes, you shouldn't have done it. But when I think back to those days, I must admit that I had been so wrapped up with the children even before they were ill, so consumed with the demands of being a mother, that I had little time left to be a wife.

There were so many times when you would come home stressed from work and wanting to talk, but I was so busy that I didn't have time—or *said* I didn't have time—to stop to listen. But I was making dinner and didn't have time, not realizing that I was so focused on nourishing everyone's bodies that I was starving our marriage.

That year before it started—I mean, between you and her—you had even suggested we go away for the weekend, that your parents would keep the children while we were gone. But I said I couldn't. I had too much to do, I told you. The children needed me, I told you. But what I didn't understand was that you needed me too.

So yes, my misplaced priorities might have played a part in what happened. Not that it gives you an excuse. But perhaps had I been more aware, you wouldn't have done what you did.

Oh, I don't know. But in any case, going out to dinner with our children to mark our anniversary was difficult for me. Not that I told them anything. What happened between us, what happened in our marriage, is my painful secret, one that I will keep forever in my heart.

As I will my regret for the role I played and the understanding that came too late.

#

June 21

Sweetheart,

Little by little, I am finding my way back. Maybe it's the sunshine that has helped dispel those black clouds that engulfed me the past few months or the start of a new season, bringing with it all the joys and fruitfulness of summer.

Or because I burned that letter—finally!—after re-reading it far too many times.

I'm sorry I found it. I'm sorry that it had happened. And I'm sorry that I let her words change how I viewed our marriage. It wiped out the good memories, tore apart the fabric that bound us together for so many years.

Perhaps initially you did choose to stay out of a sense of duty, but I can't believe that it was duty that kept you here even after the children left to go their own way. I can't believe that you were pretending all those times you said you loved me.

And I remember how later—much later—when things were very dark and we knew what was ahead, you would hold my hand and tell me how much I meant to you. That you were so glad we had found each other. That building a life together was the best accomplishment you achieved.

I have to believe that you meant it, that you weren't sorry that you stayed. That, given a chance to go back in time and revisit your decision, you would still have chosen me and the life we had made together.

I have to believe that, especially now, when there are no more choices left to make.

#

July 4

Sweetheart,

I wish you had been here to see the Fourth of July parade. You would have been so proud of our grandchildren! Joey carried the flag and Jason marched behind, banging on the drum in time to his steps.

Although it was very hard for me to listen to the sirens of the police cars and fire trucks. I used to like parades: the high school bands playing tunes they had practiced for months, the baton-twirlers sending their glittering wands high into the air and then catching them mid-fall, the excitement of the crowd as parents sought out glimpses of their children among the river of young faces.

Now, I can't bear to listen to the sirens, to see the first responders. It reminds me too much of… But never mind that. This is about the holiday that marks our country's independence, and perhaps mine as well. I feel a sense of freedom, of release, after all those dreadful months when I was chained to a past filled only with anger and regret.

Now, I can move forward into this new existence, carrying with me only memories of love and laughter, tenderness and comfort.

Comfort—that was your gift. You gave comfort even when you were the one most in need of it, something I admit I was never able to do. In that respect—as in so many others— we were a good match. Even last autumn, you were the one offering solace and reassurance to me, telling me that it would be all right, that I would be able to weather what was ahead, and that this was—how did you phrase it?—just a bump in the road of our life together.

There were times when I was angry with you for diminishing the cataclysmic event that was to befall us, befall me. It was so much more than that, I would think during those long hours of waiting for the inevitable. It was a crevasse, a fissure, a sinkhole in the landscape of our life that threatened to swallow up both of us.

But in a way you were right. Or almost right, since it was not so much a bump in the road but one of those times when highway repair crews would erect temporary barricades between the lanes, blocking cars from riding side by side along the same roadway.

You were sent to the left while I continued on the right, the wall preventing me from seeing you anymore. And those two separated life lanes never did converge again, leaving me to go forward on my own without you.

But enough of that. As I said, the grandchildren performed wonderfully, and proud parents Sonia and Max watched, beaming. Max—it seems like the business has finally turned a corner and their money woes are eased, at least for now. I'm relieved. I worried that their marriage would not be able to withstand all that pressure: the bills, the children, the fears that come when things do not turn out the way one hopes.

But when I see the two of them together—the way she turns to him and smiles, the way he catches her hand in his when they are walking side by side—I think perhaps they have learned to focus on what really matters. A lesson, I think now, that I should have learned so much earlier than I did.

As for Ben, did I tell you that he and Erin are expecting? They found out mid-May but waited to tell me until they were certain that this time she wouldn't have another miscarriage. After ten years and endless visits to the specialists, if all goes well, they will be having their first child in early January. What a wonderful start to the new year!

#

August 25

Sweetheart,

196

Good news—this time from the orchard front! Last April—that terrible month when everything went wrong—there had been a fierce storm with high winds and a torrential downpour. The next morning, I saw that one of the limbs from the apple tree had fallen, barely missing the back deck. I called the arborist—you know, the one who came out when we had that infestation of oak worms—and he cut the limb into pieces and then hauled it away.

He asked if I wanted the whole tree removed, explaining that the limb that had fallen was diseased and perhaps the whole tree was infected as well. And for a moment, I considered it.

You had bought that tree—a Ginger Gold—for our tenth anniversary, telling me that when we would be celebrating our golden wedding anniversary, it would still be producing fruit.

I didn't want to hear that, of course. Not then. It had been barely a year since you told me about her, and the wound was still raw. The thought of us making it another forty years seemed highly unlikely. And in those first few years before the tree started producing, I imagined that the apples it would bear would be bitter and shriveled, infected with the emotions that would overwhelm me every time I thought about the two of you together.

But I was wrong. When the tree finally bore its fruit, the creamy white flesh with its tantalizing blend of flavors made it perfect for the cobbler you so loved. You would eat it for breakfast and then as dessert after supper. It seemed that you never got enough of it.

You said it was like me: tart, yet sweet. And when I worried that age would make me less desirable to you, you said, like the apples, I would only get better with time, that our marriage would be all the more sweeter the longer it lasted.

So, when he asked if he should take it down, I refused. All those years when it had shaded the back of the house, all those years when its pinkish-white blossoms in the spring promised food for the autumn—how could I let one sick section determine the lifespan of the entire tree?

As it turned out, my decision was the right one. The tree had always been a good producer, but this year has been the best of all. The branches are loaded with so many apples that it will take me weeks to pick them all. And the taste! I don't think we ever had such a delicious blend of flavors.

Perhaps that storm was a blessing in a way. Had the limb remained, the infection would have traveled throughout the tree, sapping it of strength and ultimately killing it. And even though the experience was so devastating, something good came out of it after all.

(You know, of course, that I am no longer talking about the tree. But then, you always knew what I meant, even when I wasn't able to tell you. Another gift that you had that I failed to appreciate sufficiently until now.)

#

September 22

Sweetheart,

The leaves are changing. Little by little their green hues are being transformed into brilliant shades of red and orange, gold and bronze. When I look at the trees that border our property, it's almost as though there is a row of flames that promise warmth even though, with the onset of autumn, the weather has already turned chilly.

I called Abel and he brought the wood so it would be ready when I want to light the stove. Last year, with everything that was happening, I had neglected to call him in time and so went without. Or not so much neglected but hadn't yet understood that certain responsibilities you once shouldered were now falling to me to handle.

It has taken me months to get used to assuming both roles in this latest version of the play that is my life. In the early years of our marriage, I used to complain about how many responsibilities were on my side of the equation. Then once you retired, I must confess that there was more than a bit of resentment underlining my days. *You* had retired, I would think to myself, but *I* didn't. There was still the laundry and cooking and cleaning that I had to deal with.

And that was true, but what I overlooked were all those tasks that you were responsible for, both while you were working and for all those years after. Car maintenance and household repairs. Yard work and financial matters. Yes, and even calling Abel each fall to get a load of wood for the stove and the arborist to prune the trees.

Now that I am in charge, I find myself making notes so I don't forget what to do and when to do it. Sometimes I regret that I hadn't asked you in time to make me a schedule that I could follow. Or maybe the reason I didn't ask was because I didn't want to admit that there would be a time when you wouldn't be here to do them. I was never very good at that, you know. I mean, of looking at things squarely in the face and accepting them, and then coming up with a way to deal with the inevitable.

I much preferred to believe that whatever it was that I dreaded wasn't going to happen. That if I started making a plan for the "after" part, I was ensuring that the awful event would take place.

You, on the other hand, were more pragmatic, more realistic. You were the one who insisted that we meet with the attorney to update our wills. You were the one who ensured that the cemetery plots were paid for long before we would need them. You were the one who made all those lists of our financial accounts and of the people to call when something needed fixed—lists I found last April but was too angry about the letter to even acknowledge.

Now I see those lists for what they were: not just essential information but also an example of the love you had for me. You made them, like you did so many other things during our marriage, to make certain that I would be okay, that things would be less complicated or stressful for me.

And yes, they did that, yet there was one list you didn't do—but how could you?—and that was a list to tell me how to navigate this new life. How to figure out who I am supposed to be when for so many years, my identity was bound up inexorably with yours.

I know my situation is not unique—statistically women live longer than men—and yet, it is unique to me. Uncharted territory. Unfamiliar waters. That unknown place at the end of the world where dragons were thought to live. And dragons there are: fire-breathing monsters that spew flames of grief and anger and sorrow and fear at me.

And while there are brief periods when they stay in their caves and I am granted time for my wounds to heal, too often they come back out to find me. And I have to endure their attack because, really, what else can I do?

#

October 26

Sweetheart,

I went to the store today to buy Halloween candy, even though each year there have been fewer and fewer knocks at the front door, fewer and fewer cries of "Trick or Treat!" from children dressed in costumes ranging from ghosts and goblins to the latest movie character. Sonia will come with the boys, of course, but I don't expect an onslaught of little ones like we had in the past.

You might ask why I felt it necessary to buy so many pounds of sugary goodies if most of them will remain long after the holiday is over. It's because I remember those past

Halloweens, especially when the children were young. I would stay at home, handing out candy to those who came to call, while you took the children around the neighborhood.

You told me afterward how Ben would charge ahead to the various front doors while Sonia held back, needing that extra bit of encouragement from you before she climbed the porch steps to get her treats. Or maybe she just wanted a few minutes alone with you. She always was "Daddy's girl." Remember how she would trail you around the yard when you mowed the grass and trimmed the bushes?

This has been harder on her than on your son—not because he loved you less but because she needed you more. You were her guiding star, her north light. When she had a bruise or bump, she came to me, but when life presented her with challenges, it was to you she would turn, seeking advice, suggestions, options from which she could choose.

You were good at that: giving options, I mean. You never made her feel like there was only one way she could go, but rather that life was full of opportunities and all she needed to do was find the one that most called to her and take it. You made her feel like she could do anything, that she had the strength and courage and ability to succeed.

I, on the other hand, tended toward the cautious, thinking of what might go wrong instead of what could go right. We both loved her deeply, but what you gave her was what she most needed.

And that's what I need now as well—your encouragement, I mean—as I make my way in a world that seems full of ghosts. The ghosts of who we were and who we became. The ghosts of times when things were so wonderful, and other times when the pain was almost too much to bear.

And now, I must contend with the ghost that you have become—no longer in palpable form with arms that could embrace me and lips that would press to mine, but insubstantial, ephemeral, here but not here, if you know what I mean.

I turn a corner and think I catch the scent of your aftershave wafting down the hallway. I wake in the morning, and in my half-asleep state think I hear you moving in the kitchen, getting the coffee ready to brew. And the nights when I would awaken and just for a moment feel your breath against my neck, your arm encircling me, your chest, firm and strong, against my back.

All imagined, all recollections, not reality. But painful as they are, I will take those memories. They are all I have now.

#

November 24

Sweetheart,

So much to celebrate this Thanksgiving, even if there will be an undercurrent of sorrow triggered by memories of last year's holiday. Our last together, as it turned out.

The last time I would complain to you, as I had for so many years, about how hard it was to lift an eighteen-pound turkey out of the oven. And you promised, as you had for so many years, that by the following Thanksgiving there would be a wall oven to make that task less arduous.

The last time you would set the miniature Christmas tree on the nightstand in our bedroom, because you knew how much I loved having our bedroom bathed in the glowing lights as I fell asleep.

We made love that night—carefully because of the port and the incision and the tender areas on your chest that were still inflamed from all those rounds of radiation. But what our lovemaking lacked in energy was more than made up for in tenderness. And afterward, while you were sleeping, I lay awake and gazed at your face and at times, the lines and wrinkles were superimposed with that of the college-age boy who first caught my eye in Biology 101 and then my heart.

And I wondered who you saw when you looked at me now. The twenty-two-year-old bride with long black hair, glowing skin, and firm breasts? The forty-year-old mother, whose body bore the marks of childbirth? The well-past menopause woman, with gray hair, worn hands, and knees that creaked each time I climbed the basement stairs?

Years upon years, our time together like a book with so many pages that one wondered how they all could be read. If there would be enough time to go through all the chapters until one reached the final page. But as it turned out, the book was shorter than expected, with fewer and fewer lines on the pages until all that remained were blank sheets of white paper.

The same shade of white as your hair—once a rich chestnut brown even well into your sixties, but then, when it grew back after all the treatments, was the color of snow.

The same shade of white as the cover the nurse pulled over your face when it was all over. I reached out to stop her so I could see you one more time, even though you were no longer able to look back at me and smile.

I miss that smile. I miss you.

#

December 25

Merry Christmas, sweetheart!

I'm late writing this letter to you, although, in my defense, this is the first chance I've had to sit down and collect my thoughts. I received an early and much-welcome surprise last night: Sonia, Max and the twins, and Ben and Erin (now heavily pregnant) all arrived yesterday just after dinner, bearing holiday wishes and packages to open early Christmas morning. (Joey and Jason have inherited their mother's inability to wait until the sun rose for their gifts from Santa, so that meant the day started sometime shortly after six!)

I scrambled to get the spare beds made and settled the boys on the pull-out couch in the family room, leaving the tree lights on in lieu of a nightlight. And then, once the boys were asleep, and Max and Erin went to bed, the children and I sat around the kitchen table, drinking coffee, eating cookies, and talking about—well, what did we talk about?

I don't remember now since we bounced from subject to subject, although you were always a part of each topic. Decorating the tree during holidays past, with Ben reminding me of how you spent hours, it seemed, replacing burned-out bulbs with working ones.

Sonia's memory of the year you brought in kindling for the Christmas morning fire in the wood stove, not realizing that the pile held a mouse as well. The chase that ensued when the diminutive rodent tried to find a place of shelter and you tried to get to it before it could vanish into a hiding place! You succeeded, of course, but it certainly delayed our holiday breakfast!

By consensus, I suspect, they both stayed away from talking about last Christmas, and yet the memory was there for all of us. Perhaps they hoped that it would make it easier, less painful for me if the subject wasn't raised. In any case, it was well past midnight before we all went to bed. I fell asleep as soon as my head hit the pillow, not awakening until the boys came in to tell me that Santa had come and there were presents awaiting their attention.

From that point on, it was a mad rush of action: gifts to be unwrapped, breakfast to be made, the driveway and walkway to be cleared (snow had fallen in the early hours, to the boys' great delight!), and a snowman to be constructed. I loaned the twins your red plaid scarf to wind around the neck, and then took pictures of the two of them standing next to their creation.

Lunch, then after digging out the sleds from the back of the garage, a trip to the park where the snow-covered hill promised fast downhill runs followed by slow trudges back up to the summit, to be repeated time and again, until fingers were too cold to hold the ropes and legs were too tired to make the climb.

An early dinner when we returned. Then both families set off for their respective homes, leaving me to strip the beds and wash the sheets and search for any items left behind.

Now the house is quiet and dark. The only sources of illumination come from the tree lights glowing in the family room and the flames in the wood stove that Ben had thoughtfully filled with a fresh batch of kindling before departing. I settle myself in your easy chair, ready to write to you.

But instead, my mind is filled with memories of last year. Both Sonia and Ben had asked me to come to their homes for the holiday, but I refused. Just the thought of traveling was exhausting. All I wanted was to be here in our home. But when they suggested they all come here instead, I told them no. As much as I love them, I needed silence to work my way through the new reality that was my life.

I remember walking through the house, wondering what the future held for me, how I would get through all the days and nights that lay ahead. I couldn't imagine that I would survive and yet, here I am. You would be so proud of me, I think.

I went to the cemetery early yesterday morning. It had snowed a bit the night before, and when I arrived, there were no tracks on the grounds marking the paths between the gravestones. It was hard going, I must tell you, especially since I was carrying both the wreath and its holder! Twice I nearly fell, and all I could think about was how you would laugh if I landed face down in the snow, and then you would help me up, brushing the snow from my coat and my cheeks, before holding me close to warm me.

You always did find something amusing in life's unexpected occurrences, and that made them easier to bear. Even this last one: I remember you saying (after the doctor had left the room, of course) that there was no point in not smoking now, although you never had lit a cigarette in all the years we were together.

What else I remember: you wiping the tears from my face, you grasping my hands and telling me that it would be all right, that I would be all right, you saying how sorry you were that I had to deal with all of this.

But then, that was how you were.

Anyway, I managed to get the wreath firmly mounted on the holder and push the stand's metal legs deep into the ground. I stayed there for a moment, thinking back to last year. It wasn't snowing then, but the wind was sharp. I wouldn't leave until the casket was lowered into the ground.

Sonia and Ben tried to get me to come away, to get out of the cold—afraid, I suppose, that I might get sick. But I just couldn't. Not until it was over.

And since then, I have come back—at first daily, then weekly—hoping for—what? A glimpse of you hovering like a ghost? But now I know that you aren't there. Or more accurately, your body may be, but not you, yourself. Your essence. Your spirit.

That is found elsewhere. In your son's soft brown eyes and strength of character. In your daughter's tenderness and concern.

And in the memories that are locked deep in my heart. The joyous ones: the first time we kissed, the day we recited our vows in front of God and our minister, the night you held me so gently when you learned we were expecting our first child.

The painful ones: the memorial services—first for your parents and then for mine, as one by one, we bid them farewell. And the night—that terrible night—when you swore to me that it was the first and last time it would happen, and that you loved me and would always love me.

And all the other memories from our years together—some as parents, some just of the two of us. Remember the garden? When we first moved here, you had hand-dug a bed and then planted six tomatoes and as many peppers. Each year, you expanded the plot and added more and more fruits and vegetables: first a small square for strawberries, then three rows of asparagus.

That year when you planted cucumbers and squash along the perimeter… Neither of us knew that those long vines would snake out past the landscape timber to take over the yard. By the time we realized it, it was too late to change the outcome. So that summer, there was no mowing of the grass, but we did have a bumper crop of both vegetables!

There was no garden the year before last. You were already feeling the effects of the treatment, and I had so much to deal with that tilling the soil and buying plants seemed too much to handle.

And last spring—well, I still wasn't up to the task. Or I still wasn't ready to take on that final item that was for years your responsibility. Little by little, I have moved tasks from your list to mine, but that was one that had to wait.

Now I think this coming spring, I will finally do it. I will pull the weeds, hoe the bed, make the trip to the garden center, and choose the plants to set in the rows. And as I do so, I will hear your voice, cautioning me to leave enough space between them so they will thrive, telling me which plants go well together and which ones should be separated for optimal success.

And perhaps I'll even catch a glimpse of you, wearing your old flannel shirt and straw hat to shield your face from the sun. I'll see you stop to check the progress of each plant, whispering words of encouragement to them. I used to tease you, telling you that the weeds took your words to heart as much as the vegetables did, which explained why they too were so prolific. But you kept on doing it anyway.

So many memories—a lifetime of them. I don't know if I can even recall them all. But they are there, and every now and then, one will push forward, and I will see your face, hear your voice, as clearly as though you are right here beside me.

You know how much I loved you, still love you. And I know how much you loved me. Even now, when neither of us can express our feelings in the ways we used to, that love is still there. Still strong. And it's that love that keeps me going—the gift you gave to me so many years ago and the one that sustains me now and through the years to come.

Merry Christmas, darling. I love you.

ABOUT NANCY CHRISTIE

Nancy Christie is the award-winning author of the *Midlife Moxie* Novel Series, which includes *Reinventing Rita* and *Finding Fran*, with *Moving Maggie* set to release in mid-2025. She has also penned four short story collections (*The Language of Love and Other Stories*, *Mistletoe Magic and Other Holiday Tales*, *Traveling Left of Center and Other Stories*, and *Peripheral Visions and Other Stories*), two books for writers, and the inspirational essay collection *The Gifts of Change*.

Her short stories and essays have been featured in various print and online publications, earning several contest placements. Nancy is the host of the *Living the Writing Life* podcast and the founder of the annual "Midlife Moxie" Day and "Celebrate Short Fiction" Day. She also teaches writing workshops at conferences, libraries, and schools. Nancy is a member of the American Society of Journalists and Authors (ASJA), the Florida Writers Association (FWA), and the Women's Fiction Writers Association (WFWA).

ABOUT THE PRESS

Unsolicited Press is based out of Portland, Oregon and focuses on the works of the unsung and underrepresented. As a womxn-owned, all-volunteer small publisher that doesn't worry about profits as much as championing exceptional literature, we have the privilege of partnering with authors skirting the fringes of the lit world. We've worked with emerging and award-winning authors such as Shann Ray, Amy Shimshon-Santo, Brook Bhagat, Kris Amos, and John W. Bateman.

Learn more at unsolicitedpress.com. Find us on twitter and instagram.